Tales of the

MUTTERRECHT COSMOS

B. P. MEINHARDT

Find me at: pal72416@gmail.com

According to Earth's geological records,
Cataclysms occur in about 15,000 year cycles.
Last known being the biblical Great Flood.
As the Earth warms, the next cataclysm forms.

A decade of asteroid storm tsunamis began in 2026.
The Cataclysm ended in 2036, with ten-million survivors.
Since the global face-lift, a tropical water-world remains.
Mother-Sea now covers 99% of the Earth and 1% are islands.
With people and most critters, 9-of-10 survivors are gals.

Recycled is the energy of people, pollution, and patriarchs.
Plasm electron *Visitors* and microbes adapt people.
People are becoming a new species: *Gyna cosmos sapiens.*
Greenfolk skin chloroplasts feed on sunlight, as do the veg.

To bypass the next cataclysm, people use OrmNet wormholes…
Millions create tunnel-towns in many new worlds and galaxies.
Longevity exceeds 1,000 years, as people nest in new worlds.
Earth's diaspora returns to Ma's nurturing Mutterrecht Cosmos.

Archives suggest patriarchs victimized women out of birth-envy.
Goddess gals as parent teams create life with incubator births.
Patriarchs destroyed life but imagined they were gods.
Since the Cataclysm, gals and guys work together creating people.

Tales of the MUTTERRECHT COSMOS

Contents

VISIONS

On the front veranda, ma and I sit on green metal rockers. It's a cool but sticky spring evening. Ma smokes and Dad hates it. *A filthy habit*, he repeats for my benefit. Except for smoking, dad respects, loves ma. He insists I show her respect. And mostly I do.

I love night-blooming jasmine, ma planted it spiraling up strings to the veranda rafters. It's May 1952 and we're in the new house a year. Little grows in this southeast Florida sandy wasteland. Near-by tomato farms will soon give way to more cinder-block homes.

In high school, Future Farmers of America grow strawberries in addition to tomatoes and citrus. Some friends are in the FFA. They tell me that it's hard to grow anything in South Florida, unless fertilizer and pesticide saturate what passes for soil.

It's all new housing, west of North Miami and east of Opa Locka, near what soon will be interstate 95. The new homes are hundreds of concrete cinder block pill-boxes. People seem happy with their new homes. For most families it's a first home.

Talking about jasmine aroma with ma, plays tricks with my imagination. Flowering hibiscus in the sparse front yard corner looks lonely. Voicing my angst over second year Latin, ma couldn't care less. Hot and sticky dulls my senses, but dad loves it.

Constant humidity is great for mold and fungus, but not good for people. My sinus and skin are in frequent torment. Been this way since moving to Dade county. The medic says I need a drier climate. We pick snails off the coral-plastered living-room walls.

It's *God's country,* says Dad. *A cruel God,* I mutter. University is my plan for relief. Dad's God is not mine. Do loving gods dish-out cardiac death-sentences? Dad says he gave himself angina by running races with pneumonia. I learn from dad's youthful errors.

Jasmine aroma in the sticky evening stimulates my imagination. My awareness does cartwheels. The first vision is something of a shock. The vision transports me to a strange world. It feels timeless. There's an urge to record the vision.

I tell ma that I must type up something while it's fresh in my mind. Then I go to my room, touch-type on the Olivetti. It's like a dream I can touch. Vision or day-dream, it seems to be typing itself. I'm hardly looking at the keys. I've never typed so fast.

Spring break weekend and I'm typing for what seems like hours. Dad insists: *it's after midnight go to bed.* I reply, *yes sir, I'm done ... for now*. Crashing exhausted for a few hours, sleep blots-out the annoying humidity. I imagine tolerable university days in Atlanta.

Waking tired and sweaty next morning, should have put the fan on. Surprised at what I typed last night. Glancing at the typed pages, about a cataclysm. Where this stuff came from I can't figure. Maybe it's from a stressful day-dream or a separate reality.

Did the jasmine aroma trigger this vision? Reading over the typed pages there are words that I was not familiar with in 1952. Those words are *italicized* in what follows … about a future Cataclysm.

*

First vision: A 2026 to 2036 Cataclysm triggers *asteroids* and *tectonic plate tsunamis*. One-in-a-thousand people and land critters survive. *Mother-Sea* covers 99% of the Earth. Virtually gone are people, patriarchs, and pollution. But sea life flourishes.

Globally, there's 12 chains of metro islands. Montreal-Atlanta-Havana is a hundred or so small islands, totaling under a million people. It's what remains of the American Atlantic coast. The Earth's high-rise metro islands now total about ten-million people.

It's now 1,000 years since the Cataclysm ended. Matriarch stewards limit Earth population to the original ten-million survivors. With *cosmic wormhole Portals (OrmNets),* millions thrive in *tunnel-towns* of the Milky Way and *Andromeda* galaxies.

Survivors become a new species: *Gyna cosmos sapiens*. People adapt-evolve on tropical water-world Earth. Humanity transforms. It's *Insula dwarfism*: warming climate reduces body size and mass. Cooling climate increases body mass, as with Ice age mammoths.

Satellite data banks and expanding minds provide cosmic gateways, the *OrmNet Portals*. Archives suggest global cataclysms occur at about 15,000 year intervals. Matriarch stewards now guide Earth's global family for over a 1,000 years. Toxic patriarchs are long gone. Archived are six thousand years of patriarch tyranny, since the Bronze Age. Planning for the next cataclysm propels humanity into the Cosmos. Off-earth nests in new world *tunnel-towns* occur each week. Millions of people now nest in many new worlds.

Mother-Nature *Mother-Cosmos* (Ma) recycles life energy. Ma gave Earth a needed face-lift. Of ten-million survivors, more than half, the Elders, still thrive. The Cataclysm, *millennial longevity,* and *OrmNet* are Ma's gifts. Matriarchs create new worlds for people.

Matriarchs say that Ma provides direct access to our genetic code. Focusing on problems, links specific genes to conscious minds. It may be a gift of the Cataclysm, on our way to becoming a new species. Now, minds expand and deepen, as body mass shrinks.

We become *Gyna cosmos sapiens* as lower body organs shrink. But upper body, lung-circulatory system, senses, and mind expand. Body mass shrinks, height increases. Kids joke, *we look like huge stick insects*. Matriarch stewards encourage all humor.

The Cataclysm provides nine gals to one guy, for people and most land critters. *Mutterrecht* (MR) puts mother-child first. MR expands the natural inclination of all beings to protect and favor new symbiotic life. MR thrusts humanity into the Cosmos.

Mutterrecht is cosmic energy recycling on a human scale. As we nest in and explore the Cosmos, internalized MR drives matriarchs to act as cosmic life stewards. Kids call us *cosmic park rangers*. Joking about ourselves is encouraged.

Nests are tunnels into mountainous, rocky, and volcanic worlds. Fusion borers shape, adapt, and expand available caves and *lava tubes*. Each nest world is limited to 10,000 people. Before worlds are over-populated, branching to nearby worlds is encouraged.

Earth's people density is set at ten-million. Tunnel-towns are independent family clans, observing Mutterrecht guidelines to limit population. Tunnel-towns renew and protect earth-life: forests, botanicals, reefs, land critters, and sea life.

Earth cataclysms seem to occur about every 15,000 years. Off-earth tunnel-towns are solutions. The Cosmic Matriarch Diary records new tunnel-towns. Most are in Milky Way and Andromeda galaxies. But nests in neighboring galaxies are planned.
Nests manage their own numbers and seed banks. Embryo, fetus, and infant are incubated outside the human body. Shrinking birth organs no longer sustain live birth. Live birth morbidity-mortality is no longer tolerated. It was once part of patriarch health care.

*

Both of us are at Miami Edison High School. Dona and I are class-mates in sophomore Biology. We live a mile or two apart in the northwest Dade county sand barrens. We're both honor students and do well studying together. It's social dating minus sex drive.

As friends we have no inclination to play *grab-ass*. Dad says it's still dating. Lacking sex attraction is fine, says dad. Raging hormones can wait, as there are no raging hormones. While sexually attracted to gals, my hormones were never raging.

Studying is the reason for afternoon dates, but we don't need reasons. Her dad is a state trooper and that cools it for me. We like being together but don't even hold hands. I think Dona is waiting for me to make the first move. But that's not going to happen.

Since my 16th birthday dad lets me use the stick-shift '49 Studebaker. On afternoon dates we drive to Dairy Queen. We care about strawberry shakes for Dona and chocolate malts for me. We're sugar-curing our *puberty*.

Do sugar-highs dampen sex drive, I wonder? We've avoided meeting each other's parents. Our talk is about careers, school, and hot desolate northwest Miami, *home-sweat-home*. It feels like a *frontier* town. That's the extent of this area's interest.

Returning home from a late afternoon *date* I sit by the jasmine vine and inhale deeply. I crave a second vision, and soon I get what I crave. Rushing to the Olivetti, I see ma fixing supper. Once again the jasmine aroma sends my imagination off and running.

*

Second vision: It's a flash of insight. As Elder woman Lela, I'm in a circle of a dozen pre-puberty kids. We're in the tropical botanic atrium of the Jana longhouse, in the planet Ma tunnel-town. Ma circles the star Sophia, in the outer ring of the Andromeda galaxy.

The kids are in a birth training team. They meditate to the sound of water trickling thru bamboo pipes. As team trainer, Lela asks them to open their eyes and take five deep breathes, as she does the same. The Ma tunnel-town recreates a small Amazon rain forest.

Tunnel-towns on Earth and in the Cosmos take pride in recreating *islands* of luxuriant life. Earth seed-banks provide starter kits. Kits are restored once rapid growth forests are established. Propagation of mixed vegetation and small animals is a favorite pursuit.

Amazon rain forests are most popular. But Yucatan jungles are catching-on, as are mini-Everglades and Louisiana Bayous. Lately, temperate forests are popular, as are Appalachian woodlands. Mixed fruit growing groves are wide-spread in most worlds.

It's been more than a thousand years since the Cataclysm ended in 2036. Ten-million on Earth and millions in the Cosmos evolve-adapt as a new species: *Gyna cosmos sapiens*. It's partly due to *Insula dwarfism* and the vastly reduced land habitats on Earth.

Body-shrink affects our lower body organs. Lungs, heart, blood, and nerve-brain systems expand, along with extended height. Overall, body mass is declining. Skin photosynthesis now provides most of our energy, adding to our extreme longevity.

It began with Elder trials using Cyanobacteria (Cyano) chloroplast skin tattoos (tats). Now, a millennia later, Cyano tats provide most of our energy directly from the Sun or from solar radiant tunnel drones. Shrinking body mass and Cyano tats extend longevity.

Early-on, it was obvious that fetus and birth must be out-of-body in birth incubators. That's how pre-puberty birth teams began. Kids are intensively trained as parent-teams to manage seed-banks and incubator birth: from embryo, to infant, to child.

*

Lela: "Welcome y'all to our pre-puberty prep team. Y'all have a couple of years before reaching puberty. At puberty, gals and guys become birth-teams, able to donate egg-sperm, your seed, to seed-banks. But ah believe y'all know this, just making sure!

"Birthing is people-level cosmic energy recycling. I'm sure y'all heard this many times. I'll guide y'all in birth tech as part of the puberty process. Being adults means being skilled in birth tech. And going to the stars means first depositing seed to a seed-bank.

"Y'all will form birth-teams in preparation for puberty. Birth-teams are any number of people that share parenting. Teams learn and share in maintaining our numbers. Blink-on your *MindRecord* thru all our sessions, to review and discuss these sessions.

"Birth tech includes seeding, embryo, and incubator tissue culture, as well as fetus to infant tech. Parent-teams culture embryo to fetus, nurturing infants into adults. Y'all will become biologists, biochemists, geneticists, medics, and intern into parenthood.

"*Nurturing* is key. We nurture life in the Cosmos. Over 1,000 years since the Cataclysm, surviving becomes thriving. Guided by Mutterrecht (MR), we learn to nurture symbiotic life. It's MR nurture that transforms *Homo sapiens* into *Gyna cosmos sapiens*.

"Before the Cataclysm, in 1861 J. J. Bachofen published *Das Mutterrecht, Mother right, investigating the religious and juridical character of matriarchy in ancient society.* MR documents motherhood as the source of human society…." (WikiArchives)

"Nurturing life on Earth for centuries leads to longevity and mental expansion. MR nurture prepares for using wormhole OrmNet Portals to off-earth nests. As parents, we aid Ma, Deep Mother-Cosmos, in cosmic energy recycling and transformation.

"OK! Who can tell us about the origins of Matriarchy, Mutterrecht, and nurturing adaptation before the Cataclysm? Has anyone looked into the antiquity of cosmic matriarchs? And what do y'all think Bachoffen means by *juridical*?"

Jena: "As assigned study, we browse pre-Cat archives more as recreation. Longhouse stewards encourage our exploration and *recreation,* as in the re-creation of body and mind. We all study the archives, antiquity of Earth, people, matriarchs, and patriarchs.

"*Juridical* means the just and humane nature of matriarchs. It refers to nurturing and caring for people. Matriarchs are our beginning and our end, that is, if we have an end.

"Cosmic energy recycling has us studying matter, or the *Light stuff* electro-magnetic energy (emf). It's in contrast to the Dark matter, Dark energy, the *Dark stuff.* Dark stuff may be energy scaffolding for Light stuff. But the true nature of Dark stuff still eludes us.

"Perhaps Dark stuff is the geometric, structural, and substrate for emf. Is Dark stuff a geometric lattice for space-time granules of electron-based matter? There's so much we don't know, like the nature of consciousness, that most intimate experience of the self.

"Recently I found a story about patriarch victimization of women, before the Cataclysm. The story was based on over a million common elective surgeries during 2007-2019 in Ontario, Canada. It shows that patriarch victimization was subtle as well as overt.

"For male surgeons treating female patients, women were 32% more likely to die compared to being treated by female surgeons. But male patients treated by female surgeons were 13% less likely to die than if treated by male surgeons. Men were often deadly!

"Survey of the previous 2,000 years, shows patriarch victimization of women is abundantly, painfully documented. Justification based on religion is the most frequent rationale, if there can be a valid reason. Patriarchs proudly documented their own atrocities.

"As in the story about surgeons, women's hormones and nurturing are a likely explanation. In the 2,000 year period before the Cataclysm, health and medical savvy were sorely lacking, even up to the century before the Cataclysm."

Lela: "Jena, that's brilliant. Living thru the end of patriarchy, it seemed so hopeless. Patriarch greed, pollution, and violence were rampant. It seemed the only relief was a cataclysm. The tragedy is that it took the near elimination of humanity to cleanse the Earth.

"But remember, *guys are also mothers' children.* The vast majority of people, guys included, tried to save the Earth. With every meaningful effort to save the Earth, powerful patriarch oligarchs felt threatened, and violently resisted humane change.

"Patriarch leaders' fear of asteroids led to *Sky-shield* satellites, as an effort to repel the asteroid threat. But Sky-shield attracted asteroids, bringing a decade of *plate tectonic* upheaval, *tsunamis*, and finally an end to patriarchs and billions of people.

"Can anyone think of a way the disaster might have been avoided? Actually, that's an unfair question. Here's a suggestion: over the next week, until we meet again, use team search in the archives for threads of solutions that might have been developed."

Lil: "Archives show that hormone imbalance, testosterone especially, was recognized by medics long before the Cataclysm. Why wasn't hormone modification attempted?"

Isis: "That's a good point. But patriarch leaders controlled global institutions, including media and the sciences. For most men, especially leaders, testosterone levels were virtually sacred. Men took pride in high testosterone, and their manhood."

Ana: "Tampering with male hormones was considered inhuman. Patriarch leaders would have considered testosterone modification a threat to their manhood, if it were not considered ridiculous. In the patriarch *tribe,* male hormone modification was taboo."

Bern: "It's documented—then and now—how excess testosterone increases aggression and reduces intelligence. High testosterone levels predisposed people to leadership roles. Far more guys were afflicted than gals, but there were post-menopausal gals too."

Lela: "Excellent work folks. Let's see what y'all come up with for next week, same time, same place. One suggestion: look for the roots of Mutterrecht, also links between hormones and rockets. OK, get your wind-suits and follow me for some fancy flying."

*

Up at 5:30 a.m. for classes, it's late May 1953, my junior year at Edison High School. Quickly, looking over typed pages from last night, I jam them in a book bag to read later. Shave, shower, eat half an apple pie, and walk three blocks to the bus stop.

Usually, I get to the bus stop before the school bus and hitch a ride. Lots of cars are going to Edison at that time. I get there before the doors open. I'm on the outer atrium steps with others. Four or five of us *goofs talk trash* until home-room doors open.

Morning classes are Chemistry with Dr. Gibbons, Gym, and first year German with Dr. Weatherup. Easily ace these as I bought the texts and studied over the summer. The German textbook was switched, but that's fine. In *MaSprek* German I'm way ahead.

Reading my typed pages during lunch break, they read well. But it's as if someone else wrote the stuff. I hardly recognize it as mine. It's some kind of weird science fiction that makes no sense. But I keep at it to see where it goes. Is it from outside my mind?

Taking the school bus home, I do tension workouts, shower, short nap, eat then relieve dad at our toy business. Humid heat *bums-me-out*. My skin is too sensitive and body hair is especially annoying. Airborne mold and fungus are endlessly irritating.

I give dad a two hour break and do class work between customers. I like talking with customers and some are friends. Early evening, it's cooler. Sit out with ma and the night-blooming jasmine. Even with ma's smoking, strong jasmine scent brings on another vision.

Again, I'm typing with little thought, almost on automatic. Words that are new to me are italicized. Italicized words are from the 2000s, not the 1950s. Strange, how much language does and does not change.

*

Third vision: As team steward for *Nano-bot drone* code, I extend the collection net another 10,000 kilometers. The net gathers space debris for conversion in automated factory satellites. Most of it becomes *mono-molecular* film to drive Nano-bot *solar-sails*.

Coding Nano-bot drones and satellites is dull work. But it needs doing if the drone search for new worlds is to continue. As on Earth, each tunnel-town world continues its own Nano-bot search. Cataclysms are a constant threat and new worlds will be needed.

Our team is scheduled for daily *GravLev* exploratory planet charting. Teams are scheduled by HoloVid posted grid assignments. Planetary 3-D charts slowly emerge. Charts include ever-changing surface, subsurface, and atmosphere.

Planet Ma is a rocky water world half the size of Earth, with no seas. It's wetlands and mountains half and half. Waterways form global arteries. Wetlands, highlands, sub-surfaces, and even clouds are alive. Clouds contain sentient cyanobacteria-like habitats.

Early-on, Ma was volcanic, like Earth, but these now seem dormant. Conveniently, highlands are filled with caverns and lava tubes.

Tunnel-towns use fusion-shaping, rather than tunnel boring. Tunnels with native life habitats are studied but not disturbed.

Nano-bot drones are coded to look for earth-like worlds. Ma, like all nested worlds resembles Earth. Some imagine a cosmic pattern. Cosmic energy recycling favors some probabilities more than others. Is there a common cosmic geometry at work?

Tunnel-town habitats must support earth-life, or we would not be here. Nano-bots are coded to search earth-like worlds: starting with orange stars and red dwarfs. As an extension of Mutterrecht, Tunnel-towns protect both Earth and native life on new worlds.

Supernovas have similar nuclear genesis. Energy recycling is a phoenix reborn as both light and heavy elements, in the wombs of pregnant stars. Hydrogen, carbon, oxygen, nitrogen, iron, sulfur, calcium, sodium, and phosphorous are everywhere in the *Cosmos*.

Daily exploration covers 100 cubic kilometers. As on Earth, planet Ma life is based on Electrons, Viruses, and Microbes (EVM). EVM beings seem to be the energy scaffolds for all cosmic life. On all tunnel-town worlds the life forms are similar.

Ma's life is like Earths' but with distinctions: Ma's EVM life is strongly photo-voltaic, with stronger electro-magnetics than on Earth. Ma life displays high voltage-amperage. It's dangerous to interact too closely with Ma life. We keep our distance.

Life on planet Ma is sensitive, mobile, and transmits radio signals. Ma life can pick-up root, often running or flying away. Drones record instances of rapid mobility. Some life forms seem sentient, inter-linked, broadcasting at frequencies beyond our range.

With dual suns and dozens of small luminous radiating moons, daylight is most of the day. Photosynthesis is wide-spread. In caves and *lava tubes*, beings radiate light that may over-load drones. Ma people sense that some life forms resist observation.

Electro-magnetism (emag) permeates the planet's atmosphere so intensely that our *GravLevs* are never at a loss for a power charge. *Batacitors* utilize planet Ma's strong emag to power *fusion* borers in reshaping and extending tunnel-towns.

Tunnel-town techs are slow to translate life form signals. Most skilled are pre-puberty kids. Life form signals mostly resolve to *danger back-off*. Other transmissions amount to *emag caution*.

Planet Ma life along with abundant solar and lunar light, make for an invitingly beautiful life-study lab. Emag danger and fear of contaminating Ma's life keeps us mostly in tunnel-towns. Aerial GravLev surveys continue, but with limited *feet on the ground*.

To utilize their sensitivity, pre-puberty kids are now included in GravLev charting crews. Kids get in-flight by-pass coms for some areas GravLevs were about to view. When no reason is given for avoidance, drones are sent instead of GravLevs with people.

Lela's sleep provides a lucid dream of her life as a guy before the Cataclysm. *MindRecord* provides a log for the *Cosmic Matriarch Diary.*

*

Before uni, early in the 1950s, dad and I became close. Helping in the toy business gave us three years of partnership. These were intense learning years for us both. Dad loved shifting from farm and food to toy business. It was a great adventure for both of us.

The transition was challenging but happy for me and dad. For ma, it was a lonely life. Ma missed her kin in Forest Hills. Her family enjoyed a tribal closeness. For me it was a warm and comforting kinship. Ma's sisters were more like part-time mothers than aunts.

Dad grew-up on a family farm. They were four sisters and two brothers. Early in the 1930's Great Depression, they traded the farm in Plainfield, New Jersey for an auto garage in New York City. In the depression, city and farm people often traded fantasies.

Next to a major supermarket, our toy business did well. Customers were mostly veterans, young families with kids and not much money. In the sandy wastes of northwest Miami, new homes were cheap, basically they were cinder-block hurricane shelters.

Thousands of cinder-block homes were built on the sand barrens between the Opa-locka marine base and the North Miami tomato farms. Homes were on concrete platforms, with no basement or attic. Dad bought one of these for us and it was fine.

Most toy business was from the Opa-locka marine base a few miles west. Nearby armament factories employed thousands. Most customers living in the area were not much older than me. I was comfortable with the people, but not with the habitat and climate.

Working at the family business and homestead took substantial time and energy. But I devoted enough academic time to make National Honor Society and admission to Emory University (uni) in Atlanta. My health improved in the dryer Atlanta climate.

Dad inspired me academically: As a teen scholar and track star, dad over-stressed himself while ill to impress his coach. In quick succession, dad had pneumonia, scarlet fever, and pleurisy, followed by 30 years of angina, taking his life at the age of 52.

In high school I gave all of my time to academics. Not athletically skilled, I avoided competitive sports. But since age 16, dad encouraged my body-building. Body building reduced anxiety, improved health, and sharpened my mind throughout my life.

Dad's poor health was an object lesson. Growing up in farm and food work, dad loved meat and dairy. Reducing meat, dairy, and stress helped me greatly. My aunts lived into their 90s and 100s, but the uncles passed in their mid 70s.

Masturbation took the edge off my sex drive when arousal became an issue. On occasion during gym class, I'd get aroused by gals on the sidelines. Getting a hard-on was annoying with gals looking-on, but sometimes gals asked to go out with me.

Dade county had a large Latin population. Once, a couple of Cuban gals asked to go out with me and a friend. I said I'd let them know, but I never contacted them again. All my high school efforts were preparation for university and medical school.

No matter how horny I got, I took care of it myself. Politely, I resisted all approaches, until I was at Emory uni. Between academics and the family business, I had no inclination for dating. And I did not consider afternoons with Dona serious dates.

Before going to Emory there were two memorable events that dad and I shared. We enjoyed the film *Hamlet* with John Guilgud at an art theater and a Spike Jones performance at the Dade County Auditorium. Happily, we encountered school mates at both events.

I started at Emory uni early in September 1954. Along with freshman English and Chemistry, I took an advanced three-month German course, to save time taking a full year of basic German. But I didn't figure on Herr Schroeder, the instructor.

I considered myself equiped, with two years of high school German and dad's MaSprek German. Advanced German was translating the *Immensee* novella. As a work of poetic imagination, it was far more than I reckoned. Luckily I got a 'C' in the course.

*

Two weeks after starting at Emory ma phoned that dad had a heart attack and was in hospital. *Come home to Miami,* she said. Two hours later ma phoned again to say dad died. His body being sent to kin in Forest Hills, New York, I was to fly to Forest Hills.

A week after the funeral I returned to continue at Emory. Ma decided to sell the business, house, and all assets, returning to live among her kin in Forest Hills. This was fine by me. Finally, at age eighteen I was done with the torment of the Florida climate.

While grieving for my father, I continued on at Emory. I joined a fraternity to help gain med school admittance. Brother Mel helped me gain admission to the new University of Miami Medical School. But I was not keen on South Florida and finally opted-out.

Mel was a fraternity alumnus in his thirties. He lived part-time in Atlanta but spent time with me at the fraternity house. He was from south Florida, but family business kept Mel in Atlanta. Atlanta was lonely for him as his wife and kids were in Miami.

Fraternity brothers cautioned me that Mel was bisexual. In the four years of friendship with Mel, he helped me get accepted to med school. But never did he *come-on* to me sexually. Back in Miami, after graduating, I met his beautiful family.

Lucid dreams from jasmine aroma brought a new vision.

Fourth vision: As Lela, I fly four GravLevs at the same time. Each GravLev has three kids. Each kid is assigned separate but adjacent survey areas. Each GravLev pilots three drones. One each for simultaneous surface, underground, and atmosphere surveying.

Lela monitors the twelve kids, drones and data collection. The usually dense veg is observed and recorded. She logs unusual landscapes and life. An abundance of Niobium rare earth is found in a lava tube. Catalyzed graphene now replaces most rare earths.

Rare earths are seldom used. But locations are carefully recorded. Metal deposits in caves and lava tubes are tracked. Rarely needed are platinum, gold, copper, tungsten, and nickel. Niobium magnets are still used in fusion tunneling to contain the hot plasma.

In most tunnel-towns, virtually all needs are met with the transformation of atmospheric carbon dioxide. Plasma electrons and lasers are the main transformation tools. But detailed records are kept of all planet survey resources, for potential trade.

Since the Cataclysm ended in 2036, consciousness is increasingly linked directly to our genes. As *Gyna cosmos sapiens* we evolve via skin cell *Cyanobacteria* chloroplast photosynthesis. It's our primary energy source. Kids joking call us *veg-imals,* that's fine!

Cyano, Cyanobacteria are credited with the leap to complex life as Eukaryotes. Chloroplasts provide longevity, expand consciousness, and allow nesting in the Cosmos. We're both *cosmic park rangers* and *veg-imals*. That makes us serious cosmic care takers, stewards.

*

Lela meets twelve kids in training to become parents and interns. Both Kids and 1,000 year old Elders are all needed. The toxic notion that made people disposable ended with patriarchs. As energy, we're all valued parts of Ma, Deep Mother-Cosmos.

Lela: "We need to talk about longevity, Mutterrecht (MR). Before seeking help from existing parent-teams, we need to talk about goals and objectives. Suggest y'all research the antiquity of longevity and MR. The time-frame is older than humanity.

"We research archives and databases. These are the knowledge store-houses of humanity: hallucinating reality, consciousness and our sense of time. In the *infinite present*, we can imagine the next day, decade, century, or the next 1,000 years.

“Y’all may notice that our personal sense of time contracts as we age. The younger we are, the longer days seem. For kids, each day can seem endless. As decades and centuries flit by, passing time speeds-up, or at least we imagine it that way, our time shrinks.

“Time contraction becomes serious as the centuries pass. Talk with Elders about how their days speed-by. I’ve been around since before the Cataclysm. My days, years, and decades melt into each other. Increasingly, Elders tend to live in their memories.

“Talking with Elders about their sense of time may provide both perspective and sadness. Likely, it will stir-up tender and melancholy emotions. Such discussions can be painful, especially for Elders. So plan these talks with care and understanding.

“Y’all may wonder how Elders develop attitudes enabling them to go on from day to day for ten centuries. Try to understand Elder feelings, emotions, and anxiety. This can lead to an understanding of why *time contraction* becomes vitally important as we age.

“Mutterrecht (MR) directs all life energy in the Cosmos. MR guides life from plasma electrons to people, and beyond. The *Long Game* is to nurture all forms of life. MR may be considered as cosmic morality. Prior to the Cataclysm was MR unique with us?

“Searching WikiArchives, y’all will find antiquarian J. J. Bachofen introduces *Das Mutterrecht* in the mid 1800s. This does not mean that MR begins here. Anthropologist Maria Gimbutus traces it to the dawn of humanity, and long before, in all life forms.

“Folks, see if there are traces of MR in the patriarch era. Search the archives for the roots of MR. Do people begin as electron and microbial code? MR, Mother code sources all life. A mothers’ form may change but not her essence, her alpha and omega.

“Quite likely MR has no beginning. As with all life, being part of cosmic energy, there’s neither beginning nor end. But cosmic energy perpetually recycles and transforms. Is MR built into cosmic code, Deep Mother-Cosmos, Mother-Nature? Explore this!

“As y’all search the roots of Mutterrecht, think about other critters like cheetahs, mice, birds, fish, and plants. All strive to protect their kin, eggs, and seeds. That’s the ultimate goal of MR, even for people. I suggest it’s all part of cosmic energy recycling.

"MR is a cosmic force. It's the reality and presence of Mother-Cosmos in us all, in everything. Even during the patriarch era, prior to the Cataclysm, MR was a powerful force in the world. Can anyone give an example of MR in the patriarch era?"

Lil: "We browse pre-Cataclysm archives, collecting tales of heroic women resisting the *patriarch death wish.* Physicist Melita Norwood, privy to nuclear technology, protected the Earth by dispersing atomic bomb secrets, effectively nullifying bomb use.

"In the 1940s, and for 40 years, Norwood dispersed atomic bomb data to opposing contenders in the global patriarch *pissing contest.* Her actions helped insure that nukes would not be used. Norwood's efforts are an extreme example of MR in action.

"All thru antiquity mothers sacrificed themselves for children, family, and kin. Mutterrecht is embedded in our genes, realized on Earth and in the Cosmos. It's a natural condition of Ma, Deep Mother-Nature Mother-Cosmos, to nurture life energy."

Lela: "Excellent Lil. Y'all might collect these examples for a series of HoloVids, to post on the Cosmic Matriarch Diary, and on the *OrmNet Portals* wormhole network. Like Norwood, heroic women may *take it easy, but they take it.* Getting it done is what counts.

"Look into the lives of little known women. You could start with Einstein's first wife Mileva Maric', also a physicist. Did she influence Einstein? Nicola Tesla's inventive mother strongly influenced her son. Dig into the lives of these women.

"In preparation for pre-puberty training in parent tech, talk with active parent-teams. All longhouses have parent-teams in various birth phases. Ask if they could use your help, or to just observe and witness their work. There's no shortage of parent-teams.

"When we meet next week, let's talk about your progress finding active parent-teams. Most parent-teams need help. Y'all may be just what they're seeking. Your help may seem simple. But much of parenting is simple and repetitive. So start your search!"

*

Fifth vision: It's October 1954. I'm in English One, essay writing. It's my first month at Emory. Back from dad's funeral, I'm having an anxious time. Anxious over dad's death, the distractions of university are little relief, in fact I'm drowning in angst.

Sitting in the dreaded essay class, I'm startled by a foot prodding my backside thru the open back of my chair. Turning to see the source, Marge smiles coyly. At this point, I welcome any and all distractions. Taking my mind off dad's passing is difficult.

She's flirting with me. Even with my mind in a muddle, I recognize her foot prodding for what it is. After the dreary essay class we go for coffee. I need a friend more than a romance. I wonder if we can help each other in class?

Tightly wrapped-up in sadness, I give little attention to her advances. We're both anxious, she talks about her problems: a struggling mother, an absent father, and little financial support. We're attracted to each other, but are anxious, cautious, and sad.

Each week we must write a short essay. My first essay is a mess. It deserved and got an 'F.' Talking with Dr. Rouse, I fully corrected my writing. The next eleven essays were all 'A' resulting in a 'B' in the course. Marge is all 'A's. I admire her ability to focus.

Marge is also in the same freshman Chemistry class. We courted from October '54 thru May '55, until the end of the freshman year. With less passion and much anxiety, there was little hope for us. Funding, family, and academics cooled us before we got started.

Marge's ma and dad recently divorced. Her anesthesiologist ma and sole support, could not adequately fund Marge. Marriage was her way out. She married a rich guy in the fraternity next door in the summer of 1955. Marge and I never saw each other again.

The break with Marge was for me a *soft-landing*. Our clumsy relationship did not work. Rather it degenerated into a sad waste of time, for both of us. Back from summer in New York, Brother Snake told me about Marge's summer pregnancy and marriage.

Starting my second year, I began with a sense of freedom and relief. My grades were sufficient to get a small Emory scholarship. Ma and my aunts supported my four years at Emory. Aunt Ethyl sent me a $50 check each school month, so I managed.

The fraternity helped me get work selling shoes on Saturdays for the next three years. Busing from Emory to the corner of Whitehall and Alabama, in downtown Atlanta each Saturday opened a new dimension for me. And the $10 pay for the day helped.

After work on Saturday, I'd go into Grants for ten-cent cans of sardines, plus ten-cent mac and cheese. That with peanut butter and jelly got me thru the weekends when no meals were served.

During my Emory years, I maintained cordial relations with all my kin. Relations with ma remained cool. It was my fault. When dad passed I had the notion that dad preferred cremation to burial. This soured relations ma. But dad stays in my mind.

Since dad's passing, I have the bizarre sense that dad lives on in my mind. Dad guides my thoughts and actions. He monitors my perceptions. I know it's silly. Yet the idea persists with me even as a young guy transformed into an Elder gal, well over 1,000 years.

My goal was admission to medical school, any medical school would do. With that goal in mind, I pledged a fraternity to gain acceptance into med school, and it worked. Fraternity life included 50 aggressive guys in competition over four years.

My four years at Emory focused on majors in Biology and Philosophy, with a minor in Chemistry. Fraternity brothers labeled me a *grind*. Half the brothers remained good friends, but the others resented my neglect of frat essentials, such as sports and politics.

After ma moved to Forest Hills to be with her kin, she sent me a vial of jasmine oil. Jasmine still figures in my life. Jasmine was the only thing I missed about Florida. Jasmine aroma consistently liberates my imagination and writing.

*

After acceptance into the first year of University of Miami Medical School, I decided to accept a diabetes research position at the New York University Medical College. Access to free NYU graduate courses suited me far better than medical school.

Ma remarried a few years after Bev and I. Ma and I remained cool, but cordial. Unspoken, I felt ma could have done more for dad's health. Certainly, she could have stopped smoking. As my marriage grew, relations with ma became increasingly distant.

Before going to sleep I'd occasionally inhale jasmine oil aroma and find myself in a new cosmic reality. I'm never quite sure what it is. A new dimension, another world, or a lucid dream, whatever it is, I'm vitally alive but in a separate reality.

When preparing to sleep, I repeat the mantra: *Ohm ... Mani ... Shakti ... Kahli ... Ma.* It usually sends me into a lucid dream. Lucid dreaming is aided by visualizing and reciting in my mind the flowers I've lived with and loved:

Lilac, Lavender, Lobelia, Lily, Dandelion, Sunflower, Forsythia, Wisteria, Heavenly blue and Pearly White Morning Glory, Night Blooming Jasmine, Azalea, Dogwood, Cherry Blossom, Roses, Shasta Daisy, Hibiscus, Gladiola, Gentian, Carnation, Magnolia,

Gardenia, Chick weed, Duck weed, Tomato blossom, Geranium, Squash blossom, Day lily, Nasturtium, Dandelion, Iris, Marigold, Mum, Tulip, Poppy, Violet, and Butter cup.

If still awake, I visualize my earliest memories at grandma's house on Marion Street, Brooklyn. I'm four-years old again, sleeping on grandma's sofa, with a sofa cushion for my pillow, and a sofa comforter for my blanket. At the foot of the sofa is an end table.

On the end table is a Tiffany-style table lamp shaped like a royal crown, the points of the crown support the lamp. The lamp is fully enclosed in lavender, lime, and lemon tinted stained glass.

Grandma calls me into breakfast. There's apple juice, pancakes and maple syrup, cinnamon raisin bread, orange marmalade, and hot chocolate. Grandma says we'll go to the grocery store soon. But I can play now in the backyard with Skippy the Dalmatian dog.

She turns on the basement light in the kitchen and I go down the stairs, past the coal bin and up the stone stairs opening the cellar door to the backyard. First thing I see is green-wood picket fences on three sides of the backyard. These details form a religious ritual.

A cinder and gravel path from the cellar to the back fence cuts the backyard in half. Walking half-way down the path, I stop by a row of red bricks bordering the path on the right. The bricks are half in the ground at a 45-degree angle, running for six feet.

Calling Skippy, he comes to me. I pat his head and he licks my hand. Then grandma calls me to come into the house, to go shopping. Skippy runs to the back fence and starts digging. Grandma curses him for digging up the yard.

Grandma lets me hold the big cloth shopping bag with wood handles. We walk down the front stone steps. It was a sunny warm day with a slight breeze … end of May 1941. My 5th birthday is next week. Dad will come later and take me to the circus.

Big puffed-up flowers bloom in the front yards as we go to the corner. We cross to the corner grocer. In one window is a sign with a big can of Campbell's Cream of Tomato soup. In the other window are fruit crates: oranges, bananas, apples, and grapes.

Grandma buys two cans of tomato soup and puts them in the shopping bag. She buys three Sunkist oranges and adds them to the shopping bag. Gran asks me what the window sign says. I reply, *Campbell's Tomato soup*. She says, *What a bright lad!*

We walk back to her house. Cousin Irv is working on a car. Grandma says I can stay outside with Irv. He shows me how car motors work … it's with little explosions. I'm greatly impressed.

A third-floor front window opens. Cousin Jack says, *Ma, Aunt Francis made French fries ... if you want some come upstairs*. I go upstairs and Jack shows me how to use a fork to eat French fries. It's my first taste of French fries. Lots of 'firsts' today.

Aunt Francis is the oldest of gran's eight, with three kids: Irv, Jack, and Evy. Always obese, at 103 Aunt Francis outlived all her kin. They live on the 3rd floor of gran's house. Aunt Min, ma's 2nd oldest sister, has two kids, Pearl and Bea, living on the 2nd floor.

Months before, with snow on the sidewalk, Irv and Jack tied a box on a sled, and gave me a sleigh-ride on the sidewalk. It was dark and I recall the blue light of a police phone box at the end of the block. Irv drove me and ma home in his car.

Most nights, I lull myself to sleep revisiting these fond memories. My frequent return to Grandma's house is most comforting. All my kin passed-on, but they live in my memory. Gran still rocks my sister Roxy on her lap singing *Horsey-Gal.*

Most nights, my cousins take me for a sleigh-ride and give me my first taste of French-fries. Most nights, Skippy plays with me in Grandma's backyard. Most nights, Gran takes me shopping for tomato soup and oranges. And she calls me her bright lad.

Living over 1,000 years, surviving the Cataclysm, now thriving in matriarch Atlanta—still, I relive each night of these happy times. It's so typical of Elders. *Infinite present* is living increasingly in our past, while serving the present, yet anticipating the future.

*

A memory popped into Lela's head of the only violent event in her life. It was over 1,000 years back, long before the Cataclysm. At the time she was Pal, a nine-year old boy. It was in June of 1945 and the war in Europe had just ended.

Pal was walking home from school with a couple of friends. An older bigger boy was trailing behind the three younger boys. The older boy found a discarded woman's powder puff in the road and began teasing Pal by rubbing the powder puff in his face.

In a rage, Pal reached down on the road grabbing a palm-sized rock and smashed it into his tormentors head. In a bleeding rage, the tormentor was about to beat-up on Pal. But Pal's two friends held him down and yelled for Pal to run home. Pal escaped.

The next day, on his way to school, the victim of Pal's rage crossed the road to apologize for his bullying. From that point on victim and victimizor were friends. Strange that this single act of violence is so long embedded in his-her memory.

ENDERS and ELDERS

Matriarch Elders lived prior to the Cataclysm (Cat) end in 2036. So half of Earth's ten-million people live over 1,000 years. Ma, Deep Mother-Nature transforms surviving into thriving. And the *OrmNet* wormhole web serves millions in new world tunnel-towns.

Plasma electrons (Plasm) and Cyanobacteria (Cyano) enhance longevity. A Cyano oxygen revolution evolves life on Earth. Since the Cat, Cyano chloroplast tattoos (tats) provide radiant and solar energy. Skin tat photosynthesis energy is a basic longevity factor.

Long before the Cat, we've known that Plasm, Cyano, virus, and other microbes encode us. People, plants and all complex critters are more than half microbes. Our trillions of body and brain cells continue to adapt and evolve by means of electrons and microbes.

Cyano-derived Earth life adapts-evolves over billions of years. As we nest in many worlds, Cyano are found to be the seeds of life. Many forms of microbial photosynthesis are found throughout the Cosmos. The seeds of life are found even in cosmic dust.

Microbes such as Cyano and virus are the seeds of life. All seeds depend on electro-magnetic plasm electrons as the energy transfer source. To date, all the worlds with tunnel-towns and people are alive with some form of electron and microbial beings.

Most credit skin stem cell tats or *Greening,* as a key contributor to longevity. Soon after the Cat, Elders tried skin tats using Cyano chloroplasts. Chloroplasts were cultured using the persons' own skin stem cells. There was no immune rejection.

Greening provides stem cell skin photosynthesis. With extensive skin tats, energy and oxygen are provided directly to the blood, bypassing the gastro-intestinal (GI) track. In the first century after the Cat, Greening provided substantial body energy, and oxygen.

Embryo cell chloroplast DNA implants now provide full-body Greening for new-borns. Genetic skin Greening is the choice of all parent-teams. After centuries of solar and radiant photosynth energy sourcing, the (GI) track began to shrink.

Upper body: heart, lungs, circulation, and brain expand as lower body mass shrinks. Since the Cat, egg-sperm human *seeds* are cultured outside the body. Embryos are lab-cultured. Fetus to infant is incubator grown in cultured mother-uterine tissue.

Over a 1,000 years, birth mortality and morbidity are eliminated. Becoming extreme *Lifers* is part of becoming a new species. *Homo sapiens* are becoming *Gyna cosmos sapiens*. Ma: Deep Mother-Nature, our Cosmic-Mother, favors matriarch humanity.

*

Ma's gifts include *Longevity* and *Portals*, the *OrmNet* wormhole web. Matriarchs span the Cosmos with tunnel-towns in many worlds of the Milky Way and Andromeda galaxies. Ten-million nest on Earth, with millions more in off-earth tunnel-towns.

A matriarch millennium solved most basic human problems. Certainly, the 2026-2036 Cataclysm resolved major issues. But living over 1,000 years remains a challenge. Now, while our bodies sleep, we can send mind doubles to explore new worlds.

Elders, thanks to plasma electrons, can access pre-Cataclysm memories in detail. It's a virtual mems time-machine. With vivid mems, I return at will to 1941, and four going on five years. Ma takes me by trolley car to Lohman's to buy maternity clothes.

It's a warm day in May. We're on the Ralph Avenue trolley. I'm fascinated by the straw seats and start pulling out straws. Ma says *stop it*, and I do. As ma shops for dresses, I'm on the floor looking up ladies' dresses. They laugh and tell me *that's not nice*.

Ma finishes shopping. We wait for a trolley to take us home. At the trolley-stop corner a tavern has its doors open. Smelling the beer, I poke my head inside and wave. Ma pulls me away saying, *it's never too soon for you guys to think about drink!*

*

People are asked to send a daily *check-in* to the Cosmic Matriarch Diary. We can check-in via *EyeTec*, *MindRecord*, *HoloVid*, *OrmNet* or *ComSat*. We need only *Think-a-link* (*TaL*) to connect. Kin constantly check-in with each other, mostly via *TaL* links.

There's constant concern about *Enders:* the few people that tire of life after only a few hundred years. Enders seek other worlds, dimensions, universes, and a *life-after-life*. Elders living over a millennium are less prone to play the deadly Ender game.
A decade of asteroid storm tectonic plate-shifting tsunamis left ten-million Earth survivors. People and most critters are now 90% female. Ma provided a much needed *face-lift* for the trashed Earth. Does Ma consider guys a liability while gals are a necessity?

Patriarch greed, war, pollution, and over-population were washed away. Testosterone is faulted for the deadly patriarch aggression. Earth's *carrying capacity* is now held at ten-million. Ten-thousand limits are suggested for each of the many off-earth tunnel-towns.

Lifers strive to save *Enders* from themselves. It's argued that Enders have not fully trekked the free and open *OrmNet* Wormhole Web. It's a frequent point Lifers make to dissuade Enders from ending-it. Enders refer to Lifers as *salvation mothers (SalMas)*.

Most kids go *OrmNet walkabout* out of curiosity, on *vision quests,* or as part of the various coming-of-age rites. After puberty, kids mostly train as interns on Earth or aiming for other worlds. Do Enders suffer from limited imagination or a mental imbalance?

*

*OrmNet*s were activated shortly after the Cat. Before Cat, patriarchs pushed masculine rockets over feminine *OrmNets*. Blasting penis rockets was wasteful and toxic. Maybe rocket men had too much testosterone and not enough oxytocin.

Vastly more efficient feminine *OrmNets* repelled patriarch leaders. Since the Cat, matriarchs extend *OrmNets* to access the Cosmos.

Rockets that survived the Cataclysm can be seen at the Museums of Moribund Culture. The Com access code is MMC.

Direct mind to sleeper-gene links led to *OrmNet Portals*. Cells, blood vessels, nerves, plant roots, and all life derive from cosmic-wormhole geometric code. It's part of cosmic energy recycling, a form of fractal cosmic code. OrmNets provide cosmic scaffolding.

Kids think of millennium plus longevity as entirely *natural*. Persisting conditions are eventually taken for granted, regardless how extreme they may seem initially. Elder longevity must not be taken for granted. It's a gift from Ma, Deep Mother-Cosmos.

Most Elders will remain on Earth as long as it's livable. Kids born since the Cataclysm prefer *walkabout* in off-earth tunnel-towns. Wormhole *OrmNets* provide *free and open* trekking. New world exploration is a perk offered by most all intern programs.
With few exceptions, matriarchs are grateful for longevity. Personal freedom includes *ending-it*. But Lifers are determined to save Enders from themselves. Are Enders renewing patriarch thinking? Most feel a Mutterrecht obligation to preserve life.

Enders say they're searching for the next transition. Matriarchs recognize *birth-death* as a life-energy transition. In terms of energy cycles, Enders feel justified. They insist on being free to seek the next existential shift. Is that more of the patriarch *death-wish*?

Enders claim to know when they've had enough. They want to: *leave the longevity buffet before their taste for life is glutted, to make room for new kids, and explore new dimensions.* Why does this sound like more lame patriarch reasoning?

Maintaining Earth's ten-million *carrying capacity*, new births replace only those people who leave Earth. Yearly, many pubescent kids leave Earth. Most are interns to off-world tunnel-towns. And now plasma electrons can provide lucid dream cosmic exploration.

Are not a vibrant life, personal freedom, and unlimited *OrmNet* exploration sufficient longevity incentives? It's hard to understand the appeal of wishfully sought dimensions. Longhouse nurture alone should discourage *ending-it*. And mostly it does.

Longevity is a *feature* of matriarch society, not a *fault*. It extends from Earth into a multitude of cosmic tunnel-towns. Most people support the Lifer viewpoint. But matriarchs support free choice, as long as mental health issues do not cloud one's judgment.

In many longhouses, Lifers and Enders debate openly. In spite of elaborate arguments, some Enders do slip away, as is their right. Still, Lifer *gentle persuasion* persists. As time telescopes longevity, persistence, or stubbornness, grows stronger over the decades.

Matriarch nurture is deeply felt. Kin feel personal defeat when an Ender succeeds and *ends-it*. To counter Enders, Lifers constantly promote key matriarch features on Earth and in the Cosmos via *OrmNet* and Cosmic Matriarch Diary. Lifer features include:

First and foremost, *Longevity* improves people. Since the Cataclysm, health stewards optimize our genotype. Astragalus-bacteriophage transfer allows lengthening of mitotic cell telomeres, improving physical and mental prospects for longevity.
Longevity begins long before the Cataclysm. Up to the year 1900, living 50 years was considered a full life. By 2000, living 100 years was increasingly common. Dad passed at age 52 in 1954. No one anticipated or even imagined longevity of 1,000 years.

Two aunts, Francis and Hanna, and mother-in-law Ruth lived a few years past 100. These gals were inspiring. They inspired me with Mutterrecht without realizing it. Except for aunts and other kin, Social-Distancing was my life-style up until the Cataclysm.

Longevity genes as virus inhalant are adapted from Ultra CRISPR DNA of Ginko, Greenland sharks, Tardigrades, Honey mushrooms, Cyanobacteria, Aspens, Redwoods, and Bristle Cone pines. Ginko and Tardigrade DNA provide effective radiation repair code.

Second, *Cyanobacteria* evolve complex life, such as plants, animals, and people. Sentient Cyano clouds reduce solar radiation, consume carbon dioxide, free oxygen, and cool the Earth. The Cyano clouds communicate and stimulate our imagination.

Greening, Cyano skin cell photosynthesis is a key longevity factor, largely replacing GI track nutrition. Skin cell photosynth provides nutrition and increases brain-body oxygen. People greening use radiant and solar energy for photosynthesis, much as do plants.

Third, *Longhouse living* nurtures people. Attention to well-being ensures that people are valued. Shared benefits and duties involve everyone in daily living. The longhouse kinship group is a family clan. Matriarchs adapt the Iroquois longhouse to our needs.

Fourth, *wormhole web Portals* (*OrmNets*) provide extensive cosmic access. Cosmic matriarch cooperation makes *OrmNet* activation a reality. *OrmNets* allow: nesting, exploration, mind travel, vision quest, lucid dreaming, telepathy, and walkabout.

Fifth, *plasma electron Visitors* directly link minds to genes. We question ourselves and get mental responses directly from our genes. The message sent to our conscious mind in response to a question is either: *That cat will or won't hunt. Keep searching!*

Plasma energy evolves-adapts into plasma electron Visitors. It may be a Cataclysm epigenetic adaptation, preparing people for life in the Cosmos. Visitors raise our conscious awareness. Electron brain energy is a gift of cosmic plasma electron energy.
Sixth, *Mind-neurons* link all matriarch family clans thru the micro wormhole EyeTec Web, MindRecord, Cosmic Matriarch Diary, ComSat, and HoloVid Net. We send consciousness packets to explore other worlds. Our minds now traverse the Cosmos.

Seventh, *Energy* from solar radiation Dyson Sphere rings circling planets, moons, stars and deep-earth magnetics support cosmic energy recycling. Satellites fabricated from space-debris store solar-magnetic energy in satellite Batacitors (battery-capacitors).

Deep Earth tunnel drill holes provide magnetic energy. GravLev transports powered by Earth magnetics serve on- and off-earth needs. Wind, tide, wave, thermal gradient, and neutrino energy are also utilized. Pulse fusion plasma is used solely for tunneling.

New worlds are selected by coded Nano-bot drones. Off-earth worlds are nested to the extent they meet human needs. Accessible rocky mountain water oxygen (ROX) worlds are in fair supply. Off-earth nests often create tunnel-towns in neighboring worlds.

Something about cosmic energy geometry creates wormhole links between ROX worlds. It seems to be a natural cosmic phenomenon. Research suggests neutrinos and Cosmic Microwave Background radiation are involved in establishing wormholes.

Eighth, *Mutterrecht* (MR) is recognition of our link with Ma, Deep Mother-Cosmos. MR instills our dedication to life. As stewards of life, we enable Ma's infinite and endless cosmic energy recycling-transformation. MR transforms surviving into thriving.

MR drills-down to make *Base-editing* DNA adjustments for single-letter genome changes. For centuries now, we've made precise DNA changes via Ultra-CRISPR bacteria phage vaccines. It's all part of optimizing and supporting MR nurture.

Adapting to the Cataclysm, people grow tall and slim. Birth canal shrink prevents live-birth. Out-of-body *in vitro* embryo culture and incubator fetus gestation put an end to parent-child mortality and morbidity. Incubator birth has been necessary for centuries.

People increasingly resemble giant mantis insects. Greening skin chloroplasts and solar radiation provide cutin-like bronze-green skin. Changes were gradual over the millennium. It's all part of cosmic adaptation-evolution into *Gyna cosmos sapiens*.
A millennium of cosmic adaptation is partly supported by Mother-Nature and partly propagated by parenting gene technology. Matriarchs view these changes as part of cosmic energy recycling.

*

Longhouse kin often suspect undeclared Enders. Those likely to end their lives show signs: Facial muscle changes often broadcast thoughts. Increasingly, people silently transmit their thoughts. Kin may think they've provided inadequate nurturing to Enders.

Enders may be unusually: quiet, sad, chatty, or cheerful. Enders may often alternate extremes. Lifers feel morally defeated when Enders succeed in *ending-it*. It's insultingly patriarchal, the loss of a family member. And everyone feels like family.

Ender-willing, therapy starts with brain magnetics. Therapy may follow with *magic mushroom,* such as modified *Amonita muscaria* hallucinogen. Longhouse health stewards provide needed therapy. Therapy may be strongly suggested but is never forced or coerced.

Ender therapy is followed-up with Elder talk sessions, *in-your-face* consciousness raising, and hyper-imagination exercise therapy. Recent help is achieved with Cyano *cloud dreams* administered during sleep. Effectiveness usually depends on Ender attitude.

It's also been found that viewing ancient motion picture *cinemas* simulate time-travel and inter-dimensional visits. For short periods, viewers may feel transported to other times, dimensions, or realities. Multi-D HoloVid walkabouts also serve this purpose.

Water sports, muscle tension, and body-building help. Electro-mag body massage is often helpful. Full body sails allow bird-like flying, rivaling bird flight and providing long-lasting endorphin highs. Flight suits can change Ender outlook and save lives.

*

The Cosmic Matriarch Diary asks: Does Ma, Deep Mother-Nature *determine* cosmic dynamics as part of energy recycling? Or does Ma's cosmic consciousness in people provide *free-will*? Visitors respond: *That cat will hunt. Keep searching!*

Enders and Lifers often debate *Determinism* verses *Freewill* issues. Before the Cataclysm, the Cosmos was thought to be deterministic, a *done-deal, etched in stone,* or at least etched in cosmic energy. Ender debates add lively challenge to our somewhat placid lives.

No matter how we ask the question, *Visitors* provide the same reply: people may be code-determined yet consciously free. At the cosmic level determined, but locally free. It was the view of most pre-Cataclysm scientists. Now it's confirmed by plasma visitors.

Determinism code endlessly recycles cosmic energy. *Free will* consciousness as short-term decisions are likely decided before action is taken. The mental reply is always the same, either: *That cat will hunt or that cat won't hunt. Keep searching!*

*

'Is the Cosmos both determined and free?' Increasing: order, energy, heat, light, and life increase freedom, slowing entropy. All involve code, complexity, and consciousness. Matriarchs strive to *keep-the-heat,* nurturing life. Cooling and disorder speed entropy.

If electron photon *Light-energy* slows entropy, can *Dark-energy* speed entropy? Perhaps entropy IS Dark-energy? Each generation gets closer to the answers but never arrives. And Visitors keep saying, *that cat will hunt. Keep searching!*

As with Fusion energy before the Cataclysm: *It's 30 years away, and always will be.* Practical fusion was 55 years away. The same with our understanding of entropy and consciousness. Patriarch fusion and rocket tech were the result of both gonads and minds.

Dyson Spheres now use magnetars as fusion energy batacitors. The magnitude of matriarch achievements since the Cataclysm could not be imagined by patriarchs. Patriarchs were bogged-down in guy-sex rocketry, ignoring gal-inspired OrmNet wormholes.

We love these debates. Ever younger kids are contributing to these discussions. Hardly a day goes by without dozens of *check-ins* entered in the Cosmic Matriarch Diary (CMR). Some CMR excerpts follow (most comments are by pre-pubescent kids):

'Entropy increases as: order, energy, heat, light, and life decrease. Increasing entropy seems deterministic. As entropy increases, our universe seems to expand, darken, cool, and diffuse. Could entropy be just a phase in energy recycling for each universe?

‘Stars, constellations, and solar systems form from concentrating cosmic dust, increasing heat and gravity. Does nurturing life *keep-the-heat*, support energy recycling, and slow entropy in this universe? Visitors answer: *That cat will hunt. Keep searching!*
‘Large-scale cosmic and most global events seem predetermined. Regular cycles in the Solar System are predictable. On Earth, cycles and seasons of nature are largely predictable. Are these the phases of energy recycling? *That cat will hunt. Keep searching!*

‘In complex critters, an Autonomic Nervous System (ANS) *determines* most body functions. These include reproduction, respiration, metabolism, nerves, body biochemistry, and hormonal functions. Sensory systems seem to be largely determined.

‘The ANS pre-figures cell and life cycles. Automatic sensory-response systems maintain all known life. In this sense, we’re all *organic automatons*. Yet locally we exercise limited: choice, free-will, and unpredictability. Is this human scale energy recycling?

‘It all seems predetermined: Ma, Deep Mother-Cosmos codes cosmic geometry, genes, and recycling cosmic energy. Cell metabolism, energy input-output cycles, depend on genetic code. Is Ma consciously aware, or are people Ma’s organ of awareness?

‘Life depends on electron energy, of this we’re sure. Cell life energy recycles via ADP, Adenosine Di Phosphate to ATP, Adenosine Tri Phosphate, and back (ADP↔ATP). This pattern persists with some variations on all worlds we’ve nested in so far.

‘ADP to and from ATP is electron energy transfer. On Earth and in the hundreds of worlds with tunnel-towns, no major exceptions have been found. Is this cosmic energy geometry? Visitors reply: *That cat will hunt. Keep searching!*

‘What choice was there with the 2026-2036 Cataclysm? Ten- million out of billions had little choice. Did Ma hold a lottery for the *one-in-*

a-thousand earth survivors? Were gals a better life fit than guys? Visitors say: *That cat will hunt. Keep searching!*

'What of patriarch hormones? How much choice is there when we marinate in our hormones? Patriarch aggression was *influenced* by testosterone. Matriarch nurture works with progesterone, oxytocin, estrogen and a little testosterone. Hormones are semi-automatic.

'When hormone-drunk patriarchs led people into deadly disasters, hormone-primed matriarchs salvaged the survivors. For thousands of years patriarchs trashed women and the Earth. It's as if Ma's Cataclysm restored Earth's feminine balance.
'The Cataclysm was as predictable as over-population, global pollution, and patriarch warfare. It's why hormone optimization is needed to moderate humanity. Can coded virus-phage keep the balance?' These are a sampling of issues that are raised on the net.

*

The Atlanta Archive Team compiles a satellite library of *determinism* and *free-will.* Cataclysm archives are analyzed in an attempt at predictive forecasting. Archive gals replace historian guys. Since the Cataclysm, Mutterrecht gals guide cosmic life.

Archivists analyze the Cyanobacteria Oxygenation Events (COE) billions of years ago. COE was a revolution in complex life on Earth, and likely not the first. Anaerobic Archaea, sulfa-based, and radiation-energized life most likely preceded oxygen respiration.

Mother-Earth experienced many cataclysms, mostly from climate change, and assorted cosmic visitors. They initiated major changes in Cyanobacteria and microbial adaptation. When evaluating global threats, archivists analyze three documented cataclysms:

The first cataclysm occurred about 62 million years ago, ending the dinosaur era. It led to the evolution of birds, mammals, primates, and ultimately people. This cataclysm most likely was due to asteroids triggering atmospheric and climatic extremes.

Second is the Great Flood cataclysm, ending the ice-age, about 15,000 years ago. Perhaps one-in-a-thousand critters survived.

Climate stress adaptation seems to favor female survivors for most species. Most likely, some high testosterone males survived.

Survival stress favors nurturing females with sustaining amounts of estrogen, progesterone, and oxytocin. Most likely, testosterone, growth hormone, and cortisol stress hormones also increased, certainly in people, and apparently in most felines.

People adapted to-, and evolved in-, mother-centered societies. As we are born and nurtured by mothers, matriarchy naturally favors our survival. Then as now, testosterone concentrations of 25-50 nanograms per milliliter (ng/ml) of blood moderated both sexes.

Testosterone of 25-50 ng/ml remained moderate for women and elders up to and after the 2026-2036 Cataclysm. But for men, testosterone levels of 300-1,000 ng/ml destabilized humanity after both the Great Flood and during the 2026-2036 cataclysms.
Testosterone-driven patriarch aggression and fear inspired an ill-conceived asteroid repulsion network, StarShield. Developed as a hyperbolic magnetic satellite network, StarShield designed to repel asteroids did the opposite, disrupting Earth's tectonic plates.

StarShield destabilized asteroids from orbits that were never overly stable in the first place. The result was a decade of asteroid storms and tectonic plate breaks causing global tsunamis. Those ten years are referred to as the 2026 to 2036 Cataclysm (Cat).

The third Cataclysm may have been largely *guided* by Ma, Mother-Nature. But the deadly StarShield *choices* made by fearful patriarch leaders started the global disaster. These were the same oligarchs and leaders that funded military and rocket technology.

Matriarchs often comment in the Cosmic Matriarch Diary that the Cataclysm provides a fresh start for the Earth and humanity. I suppose that's true given the mess patriarchs made of both. Most likely, the Great Flood cataclysm initiated the patriarch era.

This most recent Cataclysm was partly the result of human error. Poor judgment and fear on the part of global leaders was as much free-choice as determined. Toxic levels of testosterone play a significant part in the Cataclysm that ended in 2036.

Ma was long overdue with the last Cataclysm. Would healing the Earth have occurred as a matter of free choice? Not likely with testosterone-intoxicated patriarchs in control. It's long been known that excess testosterone impairs intelligence and judgment.

Since the Cataclysm, matriarch nurture prevails both on and off Earth. Matriarchs *choose* to follow Ma's guidelines. Ma's energy recycling begins with Cyanobacteria and Plasma electrons, followed by Mutterrecht nurturing.

Patriarchs transformed the Earth into a *pig's breakfast*. By the time Ma finished the global *pressure-wash*, Earth needed a complete *make-over* and *face-lift*. By now the Cataclysm is viewed as a gift renewing humanity, as well as life on Earth, and in the Cosmos.

Before the Cat, there were millions of people, both guys and gals, doing humane work. But in the final analysis, it took the Cat to perform the radical changes that the Earth needed. Many view Ma as working thru Cyano and Plasma electron adaptation-evolution.
Ma cleansed the Earth of population, pollution, and patriarchs. Ma's survival lottery preserved *one-in-a-thousand*. The old Earth with billions, is a new *people-lite* Earth with ten-million. Survivors found high ground or were already there.

Does complex life need more gals than guys? Now, for most species nine out of ten survivors are gals. As with longevity and cosmic wormholes, matriarch minds become cosmic in scope. Many see matriarchs as the acolytes of Ma, Deep Mother-Cosmos.

Throughout the Cosmos, it's matriarch nurturing of life energy that enables the spread of cosmic consciousness. The cosmic diaspora from Earth helps expand consciousness. Key cosmic building blocks seem to be Cyanobacteria and Plasma electrons.

Ma offers longevity as a matriarch *choice*. We feast at the cosmic energy banquet, expanding mind, consciousness, and longevity.

Matriarch off-earth nesting is peaceful and respectful of life. We *pull together* for over a 1,000 years. Enders are part of this effort.

The Cosmic Matriarch Diary records few global Enders. Most are dissuaded from *ending-it*. Perhaps Enders are a moral test. Or perhaps Enders are testing Lifers. Do Enders test us all? Lifers believe that Enders have not fully considered all the life options.

It's rare for Elders surviving the Cataclysm to become Enders. Virtually all Enders are far less than a 1,000 years. Most are just 300 to 400 years, with few outside that range. Elders consider it a lack of maturity and the result of poor social bonding.

Enders may *chose* to end their stay in this dimension, while exploring others. Are Enders part of Ma's plan? Does Ma off-set human pride with a fall from cosmic grace? Or does Ender *hubris* seem like the old renewal of bogus excessive patriarch pride?

Most people consider that Ma, Mother-Cosmos has only one objective and that is to perpetually code, recycle, and transform cosmic energy. If Ma thinks, plans, is aware, and conscious, it is solely thru people and other more complex, unknown forms of life.

*

Choices that seem small can have huge and deadly effects on predetermined nature. Matriarchs have long known that excess testosterone had a compulsive effect on patriarch choices. While testosterone builds muscles and bones, excess can cloud minds.

Soon after the Cataclysm, health stewards began hormonal monitoring. With Earth's rapidly changing environment, Cat survivors experienced epigenetic adaptation. Modifications to people were both physical and mental.

In the 1,000 years since the Cat, with 90% gals and health optimizing, there's been neither war nor violence. The Cat ended the patriarch war against women and nature. We've slowly grown to realize how Mutterrecht guides complex life in the Cosmos.

Before the Cat, most all violence, war, and abuse of nature were patriarch inspired. The violence attributed to women directly or indirectly resulted mainly from patriarch societal issues. Patriarchs victimized gals from fear and greed. Gals rarely responded in kind.

Hormonal imbalance was a key factor, especially as it affected emotional intelligence. Hormone imbalance likely was a key factor underlying patriarch tyranny. For 6,000 years a Bronze Age mentality ruled the Earth, until the Cataclysm put an end to it.

Ma, Deep Mother-Nature now lives in synergy with people and all life. With Ma's aid we explore the Cosmos, nesting and nurturing life, including our own. A cosmic resurgence of sanctified motherhood thru Mutterrecht begins our second millennium.

A millennium of genetic and nurturing adaptation provides longevity and many challenging nests in the Cosmos. Nurturing and caring are our longevity *choices*. Perhaps Ma persuades people in that direction. *Persuasion* is a large part of a mothers' work.

*

Visitors are brain-resident plasma electrons. They are electrically charged energy ions. Visitors made themselves known soon after the Cataclysm. Similar to the way microbes evolve into people, electrons in the brain evolve from cosmic energy plasma electrons.

It took microbes billions of years to transform into plants and animals. And it took a few million years for primates to adapt-evolve into people. For Visitors to go from cosmic energy plasma electrons to brain neuron plasma was a matter of a few centuries.

Most likely, Visitors began the transition centuries before the Cataclysm. But the Cataclysm hastened the transition. Within a decade after the Cataclysm, Visitors were a key mental influence for people on Earth, as well as in the tunnel-town worlds.
Atlanta Elders imagine that Visitor influence began to have a significant effect first in the Atlanta islands. But all island chains believe they were first. Visitors provide direct data access to our genetic code, and provide indirect code access to cosmic data.

In our mind, we ask specific questions and Visitors point us in the correct direction to find valid answers. In ancient pre-Cataclysm

Atlanta, raising a valid point, elders might reply: *That hound will hunt*, if they agree. Or *That hound won't hunt*, if they disagree.

Since felines survived the Cat but canines did not, Visitor response became: *That cat will hunt*, or *That cat won't hunt. Keep searching!* Visitors point us in valid directions, and no more. But as our genes contain much of the cosmic code, that's quite enough.

Visitors have access to our mode of thought. They respond to our questions using our manner of speaking. Often, I ask myself if Visitors evolve from brain neuron electrons. The reply is consistently: *That cat will hunt. Keep searching!*

Careful questions led us to OrmNet wormholes, new worlds, skin Greening, Dyson spheres, limitless energy, and ultra Longevity. Becoming a new species: *Gyna cosmos sapiens* is credited to Visitors and Mother-Cosmos, along with crediting the Cataclysm.

*

Matriarchs think in terms of *energy recycling*. Ma, Mother-Nature recycled the energy of billions. As matriarchs adhere to Earth's ten-million *carrying-capacity,* births on Earth may only replace those who leave Earth. Each world respects its own limitations.

It's long been known that *energy is endlessly transformed*, but is *neither created nor destroyed.* Birth-death is merely a junction in the cosmic energy cycle. Body cells go thru this cycle many times in a lifetime. Again, it's all part of *cosmic energy recycling*.

Longevity minimizes the impact of the *birth-death* transition. Matriarchs now view people as cosmic nurturers, stewards of life. We're becoming a new species. If Ma has a program, it's to transform *Homo sapiens sapiens* into *Gyna cosmos sapiens*.

People are transforming. Most changes are adaptations to post-Cataclysm stress. Adaptations increase longevity. Most adaptations result from increasing solar radiation. Skin photosynthesis is termed *Greening*, a significant step in becoming a new species.

A dramatic Earth change is the increase in Cyano, Cyanobacteria forming clouds. Earth's surface is now 99% Mother-Sea, the global ocean. Mother-Sea nurtures sea-life to become increasingly varied and abundant. We live in a new age of sea life, algae and coral.

Coral create large reefs and algae form great floating islands. These attract nesting avians, and a large variety of sea life, especially octopus. Algae islands provide sanctuaries for marine mammals, and long-term research platforms for people.

Of the many algae types, Cyano was known as Blue-green algae before the Cat. Cyano photosynthesizers consume carbon dioxide for energy and split water usually by means of magnesium catalysts. Oxygen is the vital waste product.

Many Cyano species resemble algae, but are bacteria. Cyano and plasma electrons are the most wide-spread of all cosmic energy forms. Cyano are found in all Earth habitats: on land, sea, and even in the air. Cyano are found at depths of over a mile under-ground.

After the Cat, Cyano began forming clouds. Solar radiation electrons and sea winds provide the energy for Cyano to store hydrogen from sea water in Cyano cell vacuoles. *Waste* oxygen of Cyano photosynthesis enriches life on Earth and in other worlds.

Carbon from carbon dioxide is the *feed-stock* for both photosynth and graphene synthesis. From carbon are derived energy sugars, carbs for cell scaffolds, as well as the substrate for our material needs. Plants and all critters are derived from atmospheric carbon.

Hydrogen, stored in Cyano cell vacuoles, began floating hydrogen-filled Cyano cells into the air. At first, Cyano added to sea-vapors, mists, and fogs. Soon, Cyano-clouds formed, becoming thicker and rising higher. Cyano-clouds are the most recent Cyano species.

Cyano photosynthesis began tinting the clouds. Cyano clouds shield Earth from solar radiation, cooling earth and sea surfaces. Cyano cloud cover is increasingly sentient, as cloud color spectrum spreads. Multicolored clouds evolve into a language.

Cyano-clouds communicate with people. At first, Cyano-clouds communicated using increasingly vibrant color patterns. Recently, beautiful cloud patterns *talk* by sending visions and dreams. Cyano-clouds often appear in these dreams with a message.
Cyano-clouds seem to be a longevity factor. They stimulate positive mood and attitude, both in dreams and when awake. Cyano-clouds stimulate imagination. It's how skin *Greening* began. Dreams began to show a great variety of skin Greening.

Chloroplast photosynthesis uses chlorophyll pigment to convert solar or full-spectrum light into chemical energy for plants and animals. Greening of skin cells occurs similarly as Cyano plasma membrane uses chloroplasts, with no rejection in either.

Greening became a fashion as Cyano chloroplasts proved viable in skin cells with micro-needle tattoos (tats). Cyano tats exposed to solar or radiant light provides photosynthesis, increasing body: energy, oxygen, and tolerance for solar, and non-solar radiation.

Adapted chloroplast virus phage provide skin cell acceptance of Greening. Beginning with skin stem cells, acceptance of Greening chloroplasts is far better than the acceptance of pre-Cataclysm tattoo dyes. Greening is a key factor increasing longevity.

Sunlight converts carbon dioxide and water in chloroplasts to carb-sugar energy, usually with magnesium ion catalysts. Green energy is Adenosine Tri Phosphate (ATP) and nucleic acid synthesis of Nicotinamide Adenine Dinucleotide Phosphate (NADP).

Providing plant cell energy, chloroplasts function much like animal cell mitochondria power supplies. In addition to photosynthesis, chloroplasts synthesize fatty acids and amino acids for needed proteins, cell energy, and immunity factors.

Depending on tattoo size and the number of chloroplasts, oxygen availability may increase for the entire body. For the upper body, greening tats significantly increase brain nutrients and oxygen for increasing mental function.

Mental processes gain, and also under-sea respiration. Long term greening thickens and strengthens skin to a chitin-like texture. Skin tone takes on a near metallic bronze glow. Skin greening is now considered a sign of beauty. Most people are into it.

Mitochondria-chloroplast compatibility, function, and morphology seldom are a problem. Both generate cell energy and both have their own DNA. For both, ATP↔ADP is the electron energy source. Plasma electrons are basic to all known cosmic life forms.
Greening is well accepted. Allergic rejection is rare. Virus phage anti-rejection vaccine renders chloroplast plant protein well accepted in the few people with resistance to Greening.

Solar, radiant, and chemical energy provide the electron ionization energy for both chloroplasts and mitochondria. Protein immune compatibility needed some adaptation via virus phage, but now mitochondria and chloroplast symbiosis are virtually complete.

*

At puberty onset, kids tower over six feet. And post puberty kids shoot up past seven feet. Greening energy efficiency keeps people trim. People grow tall and slim, as lower body organs shrink. These changes, especially skin Greening, contribute to longevity.

Since live birth became a deadly option, culturing out-of-body embryo fetus incubation now provides 100% viability. Relief from birth mortality-morbidity impacts overall longevity. Parent-team anxiety still exists, but large parent-teams reduce overall anxiety.

Before the Cataclysm, 50% or more live birth mortality and morbidity were common. Caesarian birth increased. With the Cataclysm, total external embryo-to-fetus incubation became necessary, as narrowing of the uterus became widespread.

Two surprising results of external incubation further improve longevity. First, mitotic cell telomeres are lengthening. And second, total body cell recycling now occurs in under two years. Before the Cataclysm, full cell recycling took five-to-seven years.

Matriarch technology fully eliminates birth pain and suffering, even with some parent team angst. Encouraging large parent birth teams greatly reduces birth stress. The key is sharing *eyes-and-hands-on* attendance with more people in parent team birth shifts.

Some anxiety aids birth team attention, caution, and perseverance. Additional cortisol stress hormone, experienced in birth teams, sharpens sensitivity and alertness. But it has long been known that larger birthing teams substantially reduce work load anxiety.

When longhouses lose a person, for whatever reason, parents at the top of the birth list are alerted to form a birth-team. Parent teams may be dozens or an entire longhouse of kin and mates. Parent teams are trained by Elders, stewards, and experienced parents.

Parent teams rotate shifts since gestation may be five months. Gestation service is a 24/7 process. Two-hour shifts are attended by at least two team-mates. Birthing is an intensely serviced longhouse activity. And there are seldom enough team parents.

Birth vigil check-lists of tasks are complex. Shifts include: monitoring metabolism, fetal massage, sensory stimulation, talk and music sensitization. Backup embryos are cultured in case of primary embryo failure. In this way there are no birth loses.

Birth teams provide continual fetal monitoring. Virus phage gene repair is provided as needed. Parent teams master gene repair and modification. Parents become genetic engineers. Ideally, parent teams are an entire longhouse of about 100 people.

With the need for round-the-clock incubator birth attendance, the more people scheduled, the better for the child. If two people attend at each two-hour shift, in a 100-person longhouse, each person will attend for only two-hours in every 48-hour period.

Egg mothers provide needed cell tissues for culturing live-cell incubators. These are live-cell linings of incubator wombs. Backup womb tissues are also cultured. Egg-mothers and Sperm-fathers are birth team stewards, within the kinship longhouse.

External incubator fetus gestation facilitates genetic optimizing and population planning. The main task of puberty rites is supplying ova-sperm to seed-banks. Like insects, post puberty kids produce viable egg-sacks for harvest at two or three year intervals.

Longhouses maintain their own seed-banks and incubators. This is the case on Earth and in off-earth worlds. Seed-banks consist of trehalose-sugar stasis units. Vegetable trehalose sugar prevents drying and freezing. Trehalose supports inter-stellar seed travel.

Trehalose is a natural glucose sugar. In nature, it preserves insect cocoons from desiccation. Before the Cataclysm, a method was developed using trehalose to indefinitely preserve sperm and eggs at ambient temperature and pressure.

*

Kids jokingly call each other *mantis folks* and *stick insects*. Our mantis-like body emerges as matriarchs adjust to the stress of a changing Cosmos. We grow tall and slim. Our heads become large ovals. Greening as chloroplast skin tats accelerates the transition.
As most of us have gone Green, our skin texture is like insect cutin. To one degree or another, the vast majority of people have adopted Greening. Over the centuries, the benefits of Greening have proven overwhelming. Elders especially pioneered Greening.

Most people value the trend started by Cataclysm adaptation and continue to proceed along the same lines. We embrace our mantis-like adaptation. We're encouraged to joke about it. Gradual adjustment over centuries renders Greening adaptation negligible.

Matriarch stewards encourage laughing at ourselves. Our mantis-like transition is a constant source of amusement. Matriarchs delight in the comic relief constantly provided by Ma, Mother-Nature. Human artifices merely advance what Ma provides.

Laughing at ourselves supports our longevity feedback loop. All the longevity enhancements since the Cataclysm are adaptations to the changing Earth and Cosmos. Cosmic energy recycling plays out locally as the perpetually changing dynamics of life.

Earth warms, Mother-Sea rises, and the land diminishes. But life in Mother-Sea thrives. As Cyano clouds moderate solar warming, vitality is added to life on Earth and in the tunnel-towns. Earth is globally tropical but livable, and we strive to keep it that way.

Earth and Moon Dyson Rings expand by storing and relaying solar energy. Increasingly, Dyson Ring satellites and Cyano clouds divert solar energy that would overheat the Earth. Similarly, the off-earth worlds have either added or plan to add Dyson Rings.

Ma will eventually provide another face-lift for Mother-Earth. Sooner of later, regardless of what we do to avoid it, there will be another cataclysm. That's something we can count on, and plan for. Tunnel-towns will continue to be added in all new worlds.

On Earth, tunneling under Mother-Sea compensates for lost land. Tunnel-towns now expand island area ten-fold. People, especially kids, explore new worlds in tunnel-towns all over the Cosmos. For seed donor kids, fusion tunnel skills are a favorite intern pursuit.

Algae form *Floats*, large floating islands with semi-permeable graphene mats. Many *Floats* support live-on research stations. *Float* stations also prepare kids as marine interns. Coral reefs grow off most islands. Reef-Float HoloVids are becoming an art form.
For hundreds of years, Cyano hydrogen vacuoles formed ever larger clouds. Cyano clouds blanket Earth, absorbing much of the Sun's radiant energy. With Cyano cloud solar energy capture, Earth's climate is fine-tuned to reduce heat and storms.

Sentient Cyano clouds resemble huge multi-colored brains. Links between clouds and people are increasing. Lucid dreams are sent to the Cosmic Matriarch Diary. Cyano cloud dreams function as do the Visitors, providing a creative direction to our imagination.

*

Island chains are high rise metros. Some metros rise from slow tectonic plate up-thrusts. Skin Greening is almost total. And Greens turn tunnel-towns into botanical art. Duplicating Sun and Moon phases, tunnel drones fine-tune climate and daily cycles.

Botanical culture as an art form provides both mental stimulation and peace of mind. People and plants seem to culture each other. In particular, plant culture develops nurturing skills. Veg juices, tonics, ferments, and teas supplement skin Greening nutrition.

Plant pigmentation is carefully studied and archived. Green pigmentation is especially varied and categorized. Tunnel-town botanicals provide an endless delight. Pigment shades, tones, and textures in the Cosmic Matriarch Diary now total over a thousand.

Pigment chemistry is widely pursued on Earth and in most off-earth worlds. Pigments are mainly agents in photosynthesis. Chlorophyll, xanthophyll, carotene, and other pigments found on Earth are similar to those on other worlds.

Xanthenes and carotenes are especially interesting. Natural pigments such as cantha-xanthene found in mushrooms, spinach, and flamingo feathers provide a nutritional tomato-red. Crypto-xanthene is a translucent to white pigment.

*

The Sophia clan is the Atlanta portion of the Montreal-Atlanta-Havana metro islands. Earth metros tunnel extensively under Mother-Sea to expand surface area and for security. The Cataclysm teaches the value of tunneling, among many other lessons.

Helsinki metro islands rise, linking Copenhagen to the Dublin-Cork metro islands. Denver-Frisco-Vancouver are rising. Earth's tectonic plates are dynamic, as is the Cosmos. Tunnels, algae floats and OrmNet wormholes expand life and people in the Cosmos.

We say there's more life in the tunnels than under Mother Sea. Skin Greening aids in adapting to life in Mother-Sea. Becoming *Gyna cosmos sapiens* has us wondering what's next. We see ourselves as vital parts of cosmic energy recycling.

Cyano clouds provide dream-like images, stimulating imagination to create new realities. Cyano clouds together with Dyson satellites send solar energy by both laser-pulse and long distance electro-magnetic radio frequencies (emf).

Plasma *Visitors* link Cyano emf consciousness to sleeper-genes. Direct mind to gene links initiate surges in art and science. People of Earth become people of the Cosmos. Cyano travel the Cosmos. And as the children of Cyano, now we also travel the Cosmos.

Asking ourselves specific questions, Visitors reply in our mind. Asking if Cyano emf link conscious mind and sleeper-genes, the reply is positive: *That cat will hunt. Keep searching!*

Matriarch longevity is in the infinite present. Adapting to the wormhole web network, people become cosmic stewards. Our goal is to extend nurturing care to all symbiotic life. People are transformers and are transformed in cosmic energy recycling.

Analyzing pre-Cataclysm social-political movements, the Atlanta Archive team notes in the Cosmic Matriarch Diary: progressive patriarchs attempted to extend family nurturing globally. In spite of overall failure, there were some isolated pockets of success.

Unitarians, socialists, various communists, and assorted communalists attempted global family. Hutterites, Mennonites, Amish, Buddhists, and Bruderhof had some success. With patriarchs and the Cataclysm, it all came to an end.

Now, with matriarch guidance and no patriarchs, the Mutterrecht cosmic family becomes a reality. Aided by Mother-Nature and Cosmic Consciousness, matriarchs nest in many worlds. People adapt to the changing Earth, and to a Cosmos in dynamic flux.

Living over a thousand years since Cataclysm is a cosmic achievement. Kids born since the Cataclysm take it for granted. They go on cosmic *Walkabouts* and *Vision Quests*. Many kids are cosmic explorers, always on the move, and that's fine.

Plans are to send Nano-bot drones *into* stars. As Star-bots, they'll attempt to create magnetic tunnels in stars. That's inspired by the magnetic toroid mirrors created for fusion tunneling. The hope is to harness solar corona energy to power wormhole expansion.

Can nano-size Star-bots survive solar coronas if protected by magnetic toroids? Sending millions of robots the size of bacteria, protected by magnetic toroids, does not insure any will return data. But of course it will be attempted. And why not?

*

And what of the Enders? Do Enders experience biochemical or hormonal changes? What are the prospects of finding *after-life* dimensions, as Enders so fondly hope? Visitors asked about these issues give hopeful replies to Enders. That's part of the problem.

Soon after the Cataclysm, organic-electron body radiation and electron potential monitors were developed. Bacteria-phage genetic vaccines provided internal monitoring and normalizers. Phage provide internal self-correcting immune system feed-back.

Most Enders submit to phage and Visitor probing. Enders consistently prove as normal as other people. Visitor probing suggests that Enders pursue a *separate reality*, removed from the pursuits of most people. Some Enders are doing phage research.

Phage function as virus-size factories for optimizing longevity, especially immunity and brain neuron functions. Phage modify specific genes to add, modify, or remove at a molecular level. Phage may also modify genes of mitochondria and chloroplasts.

Enders usually agree to a full body analysis. They're aware that imbalances of hormones or neurotransmitters can influence judgment. As all do, Enders strive to avoid ills. They may hope for *alt-dimension after-life*, but still crave a degree of assurance.

Hormones that typically become unbalanced include: vasopressin, cortisol, testosterone, estrogen, progesterone, oxytocin, insulin, and growth hormone. But not necessarily in that order. Monitoring implants or patches usually detect imbalances, but not always.

Hormones may affect and be affected by neurotransmitters such as serotonin, dopamine, endorphins, adrenalin, and norepinepherine.

Balances of these help to maintain a positive mood. Persistent low levels may cause anxiety, depression, also Ender suicidal thoughts. Natural body endorphin opioids are secreted by the pituitary. Endorphins relieve pain by raising pain thresholds. And produce euphoria by means of exercise, laughter, also apple and other fruit peels that contain *ursolic acid* and *theobromine*.

Enders are more curious than suicidal. They're influenced by tangible data. With few Enders, there's few Ender bio-assays. But the few bio-assays reveal normal biochemistry. Possibly, Ender views approach the cutting edge of mental development.

About *life-after-life* and *near-death*, there are thousands of pre-Cataclysm reports, and all are suspect. If hard data about anticipated Ender destinations exist, they're not shared. New dimensions are scarce, far harder than finding new cosmic worlds.

Open-ended longevity is a common expectation, but death and even near-death are rare. Intense curiosity is also reasonable, and is shared by many. We pose these questions in our mind: Is there *life-after-life* and dimensions beyond those we know well?

Visitors say: *That cat will hunt. Keep searching!* Cosmic Matriarch Diary flows with views on Cosmic Consciousness, Energy Strings, Quantum Gravity, and even Slowing Entropy, but *near-death* comments are hard to find. Our longevity may discourage it.

Enders are usually persuaded to research the various options before making what may be an irreversible decision. *Walkabout* thru the OrmNet wormhole web is encouraged to provide clues. Wormhole *walkabout* often satisfies Ender curiosity, or just exhausts it.

All we can do is persuade, provide empathy, and reason. But some Lifers are determined. They will not make it easy for Enders. It's become something of a quest for both Lifers and Enders. It's a constant challenge and *Ma knows* that we need challenges!

Perhaps Enders provide a needed challenge. But all threats to survival must be challenged and carefully analyzed. Perhaps Enders exist just to give Lifers a challenge. Some stewards are concerned that Enders are creating *creeping patriarchy*.

After all, planning for the next cataclysm is hardly a real and present challenge. The threat that Enders present is the closest we come to actual danger. And what about elusive complex beings on tunnel-town worlds that are hidden? They may or may not exist.

MILLENNIALS

Atlanta matriarchs send millennial greetings: *From surviving, to thriving, and nesting throughout Mother Cosmos. Where has the matriarch millennium taken us, and where are we headed? Her-story continues one thousand years after the Cataclysm (Cat).*

It's a thousand years since the asteroid storms ended in 2036. The new Lunar year is 1,000 AC (After Cat). The old Solar year is 3036. As before the Cat, each year thousands of small asteroids, or bolides, continue to fall into Mother-Sea, adding mass to the Earth.

On Earth, we limit our number to ten-million. There are millions more in many new worlds. Of the billions prior to the asteroids, *one-in-a-thousand* survived on a few metro islands. Metro islands survived the tectonic plate ruptures and ten years of tsunamis.

Millennial Elders are half of the thriving Cat survivors. *Her-story* is at least a million years of mothers nurturing people and life. A sparsely peopled Earth preceded *His-story* of the Bronze Age and 6,000 years of patriarchy, over-population, and Earth-trashing.

*

Now, all Elders are asked to add their millennial stories to the Cosmic Matriarch Diary or the Wormhole Network Web (OrmNet). Personally, I've had more than 1,100 years. Longevity is valued, but now it's largely taken for granted, especially by kids.

Born a guy in 1936, my first century was lived as a guy until the Cat ended in 2036. Even before the Cat, I satisfied my life-long desire to be a gal. Key changes began naturally in my hundredth year, as I adapted to the stress of the Cataclysm.

By my first 100 years I'd become a gal. As a child, I was lovingly nurtured by my aunts. I always preferred gals, and *social-distancing* with guys, even before the Covid pandemic of the 2020s. My life-long attraction to gals is sexual, cultural and social.

With no special talents or skills, I was and still am attracted to ideas and flights of imagination. Early-on, my interest in medicine was largely due to my father's long-term angina heart disease. I was 18 when dad passed, starting at Emory University (uni).

Philosophy, Biology, Chemistry, Economics, Networking, Coding, and Cosmology remain my interests. While admitted to medical school, I decided on medical *research*, not medical *practice*. During this time I chased ideas, both in and out of the sciences.

In my heart of hearts, I suspect that patriarch misogyny and victimization of women, was a matter of deep-seated envy. The ability to bear eggs and nurture new life places women in the heavens as mother goddesses. Women create life, men do not.

My focus, affection, and interest has always been gals. Love for gals began with ma, aunts, wives, and assorted female kin. Yet for anyone who would listen, ma repeated her story of my painful birth. I loved ma, but there was a life-long coolness between us.

When dad was laid-out for viewing at the funeral, ma complained that dad did not look shaved. But dad was shaved that morning. Hair cells continue to grow long after most body cells die. I never forgot that. Ma loudly and often found fault with trivia.

From my earliest years, ma retold her story of my painful birth. Loving ma, most of my affection was for dad. Ma was skilled at drilling me in basic education: spelling *capa-city* at eight. Dad encouraged my science explorations and language studies.

Over a 1,000 years, I've grown to resemble Lela my wife of over 40 years. Matriarch tech made it possible. Lela was both loving and adventurous. She acted out what I could only imagine. In my memory, I honor Lela and all the gals that created me.

*

Before the Bronze Age, human culture was mother-centered, as it was after the Cataclysm. Now a water world, Earth supports the original ten-million. But off-earth tunnel-town worlds with 10,000 people each, now total many millions in hundreds-of-worlds.

Ma, Mother-Nature nurtures nine gals to one guy, for people and most all land critters. Since the Cat, most land life follows this nine-to-one pattern. It's an adaptation to a new tropical Earth. Even before the Cat, the number of females exceeded males.

It's called *Insular dwarfism* and it changes island critters. Island critters have reduced body mass. People resemble seven-foot mantis insects. As height increases, body mass declines. By the time kids reach puberty most are slim and over seven feet.
As lower organs shrink, brain, heart, circulation, and lungs expand. Birth organs began shrinking soon after the Cataclysm. The danger of *live-birth* requires egg-sperm seed-banking at puberty. Embryo, fetus, and infant must be cultured and incubated outside the body.

Over the millennium, matriarchs replace only those leaving Earth to off-earth tunnel-towns. Earth's original ten-million Cataclysm survivors thrive. Off-earth *nests* max-out their numbers at about 10,000 before branching to new worlds.

Admittedly, our model has been the pre-Cataclysm Hutterites of western Canada. When Hutterite communities reached an excessive number of people, ships were chartered to send people and equipment, usually to Central or South America.

On and off-earth, all births are via incubator. Kids train in birth tech for two years prior to puberty. Puberty is achieved when kids can donate viable egg and sperm to seed-banks. Kids then form parent teams, but must wait for a vacancy to get the parenting call.

Birth teams consisting of an entire longhouse may train as birth parents. A mothers' uterine tissue is cultured to line incubators. Parent teams schedule and work all aspects of birthing, from embryo culture to fetal monitoring, and infant to child nurturing.

Before the Cataclysm (Cat), birth mortality of over 50% was common. Birth mortality-morbidity and the victimization of women were part of patriarchy. But since the Cat, with incubator birth, birth mortality-morbidity is completely eliminated.

*

The Cataclysm decade included asteroid storms and plate tectonic tsunamis. With people, *one-in-a-thousand* land critters thrive. Ma, Mother-Cosmos provides the global sea with an abundance of life. Ma recycles, transforms all cosmic energy, including the Earth.

Earth is a life-supporting tropical water-world. Cataclysm's face-lift cleansed Mother-Earth of population, pollution, and patriarchs. Ten-million Cat survivors are maintained as the limit of Earth's human *carrying capacity*. These limits are part of Mutterecht.

With tunnel-towns, floating algae islands, and wormhole OrmNet diaspora, matriarchs anticipate the next cataclysm. On Earth there are records of cataclysms every 15,000 years, or so. Survival preparations are part of Mutterrecht, as matriarch cosmic nurture.
Continents sank below Mother-Sea. Linked are Montreal, Atlanta, and Havana islands. Vancouver, Frisco, Denver, and Mexicali islands are also linked. Except for Atlanta islands, the rest of North America, between Montreal and Havana is under Mother-Sea.

Lhasa, Sidney, and the rising South Pole islands remain. Dublin, Helsinki, Copenhagen, Barcelona, and Bilbao are remaining metro Euro islands. Other flourishing island chains include Crete, Cyprus, Haifa, Istanbul, and Jerusalem-Tel Aviv.

Pre-Cataclysm Atlanta hills are now islands in tropical Mother-Sea. Sonar pulverized paving provides coral reef starter. Atlanta isles are restored to botanical splendor. *Soil liberation* opened the land to a wide array of plants and supporting critters.

Greens, as skin chloroplast pioneers, view Cyanobacteria (Cyano) as the *Earth mothers* of complex life. People, plants and all critters evolve and adapt from Cyano. Cyano spores are cosmic travelers. Cyano-like microbes are found on most tunnel-town nest worlds.

*

Soon after the Cat, Elders began experimenting with body *Greening*. Using a person's skin stem cells adapted to Cyano, techs tried Cyano chloroplast skin tattooing (tats). Photosynthesis tats first were an Elder fashion, and later a longevity option for all.

Using a person's own skin cells avoids *Greening* rejection. Now *Greens* may be nasal mist-vaccinated with Cyano-phage virus. Compatibility was proven between stem and receiver cells, in regard to peptide proteins and related immunity factors.

Nasal vaccine bypasses the brain-body blood barrier, allowing T-cells to find Major Histo-Compatibility (MHC) antigens. Starting with a person's stem cells, chloroplast rejection is rare. Skin tats are still a popular way to maximize body *Greening*.

Initial *in vitro* lab dish stem cell chloroplast cultures showed no sign of rejection. In sunlight, Cyano chloroplasts perform varying amounts of photosynthesis. Bypassing the gastrointestinal track for body energy provides a *great leap forward* in longevity.

In vivo volunteers with small chloroplast skin micro-needle patches easily tolerated the first Greening tats. Eventually, Cyano virus phage were cultured to safely and efficiently deliver chloroplasts as *Greening* tats, over major expanses of the body.
Over the millennium, skin *Greening* gene transplant is included as a part of parent-child birth tech. Strange that much of the tech for *Greening* was obtained from WikiArchives. It was gleaned from satellite data stores originating long before the Cataclysm.

A 1,000 years later, the people on Earth and in the Cosmos, obtain much of their oxygen and energy from *Greening*. We're becoming a new species *Gyna cosmos sapiens*. Now we feed on solar energy via photosynthesis, much as do green plants.

Atlanta islands are botanical wonders. Earth islands outdo each other in the variety of life. GravLev floater tours visit lush parks, mini-forests, and coral reefs. As body *Greening* is wide-spread, Greening Earth and off-earth tunnel-towns is also a passion.

Dwarf buffalo grass (Logras) paths replace paving. Adapted to tropical Earth, spreading is limited by kudzu and sea water. Logras and kudzu are often juiced and fermented. In taste and nutrition, the two greens are a taste blend of rosemary, celery and cilentro.

Georgia Tech, Emory, Fisk, and Spelman schools still research: *Greening*, wormholes, and all-surface GravLev floaters. Wind, wave, tide, deep-earth magnetics, solar, and Dyson spheres also supply energy. Plasma electron *Batacitors* store most energy.

GravLev floaters eliminate the need for paved surfaces, providing land, sea, tunnel, and air travel. *Monos* are quantum magnetic monopoles providing GravLevs with gravity-free power. Mono-adapted ancient auto *ReFits* become all-surface GravLev floaters.

Monos also power graphene flying-suits for bird-like flight. Kids compete with gulls and each other. Matriarch stewards insist: all flying-suit air-racing and acrobatics must be over open water.

*

Atlanta gals took charge during and after the Cat. Gals organized neighbor teams. Where were the guys? Most guys were missing. Nine out of ten Cat survivors were gals. A 1,000 years later, that ratio continues. Most land and sea life is now 90% female.

For most Atlantans, the shore is a short grassy walk. With land and sea now at relative peace, calm envelopes Atlanta's island-hills. Soft sea breezes and gentle surf support islander contemplative consciousness. Habitats now include land, sea, air and tunnel-town.

People still comfort each other as they watch kids at play. For most kids it's a fun day at the shore. And for the island hills of Atlanta, living in tropical Mother-Sea provides a pleasant life at the sea-shore. Virtually all of Atlanta is now the *shore.*

Com stewards hype Earth as a tropical wonderland. Satellite links reveal the challenging reality. As most sea veg is edible, algae processing was an early activity. Now with *Greening*, algae juices, ferments, teas, and tonics are widely consumed supplements.

Greens say, *like plants, we learn to thrive where we're planted, or not!* People learn to live on land, in sea, in tunnel-towns, and in the air, energized by *Greening* and green fluids. For Greens, tunnel-town drones effectively simulate radiant sun and moon.

Soon after the Cataclysm gals aided all in need, as most guys were gone. Male morale collapsed early-on. For gals it was another day of *keeping-it-all-together*. It's like it was before the Great Flood. For over a millenium, Mother Earth has been cleansed of toxins.

After the Cataclysm gals shared all resources. Longhouse shared-living arose as buildings decayed. Post-Cataclysm Mutterrecht is *shared needs and deeds*. A unified Earth family is the first goal, extending humanity via wormhole OrmNet into the Cosmos.

Atlanta's health and education community formed rescue teams. Responders were medics, researchers, academics, instructors, teachers, trainers, students, alumni, and kin. Schedules and shifts were activated as needs were met.

Gals were steeled to disaster since the 1865 *Siege and Burning of Atlanta*. It's etched in women's hearts and minds. Guys are only a tenth of the people now. And all people now share equally. All realize that *guys are also mother's children*.

Underground Atlanta survived largely intact. But most of Five-points low-lands, to the ancient rail terminal is coral reef. The hill parks, libraries, Atlanta Parthenon, and Fox theater are preserved. Pre-Cataclysm patriarch distortions are corrected.

The Atlanta Parthenon now includes the Forum of the Matriarchs. These are 4-D HoloVids of Isis, Lilith, Athena, Diana, Pelasgian and Amazon Venuses, as well as women who sacrificed for people and the Earth. Every hour goddesses and matriarchs come alive.
The Cyclorama-Civil War Museum is now part of the Atlanta Parthenon. *Her-story* is the main feature of the pre-Cataclysm Cyclorama. Now it's Atlanta women, from Cataclysm to cosmic diaspora, a millennium nurturing life on Earth, and in the Cosmos.

*

A thousand years later, a leaner but longer-lived humanity nests in the Cosmos. Over the millennium, *Homo sapiens* become *Gyna cosmos sapiens*. Ma, Deep Mother-Nature, our Cosmic-Mother gives provides cosmic energy to perpetually recycle all life.

Some say, *the billions who passed-on are the lucky ones*. Along with people, *one-in-a-thousand* land critters won the survival lottery. Life thrives on Earth and in the multitude of tunnel-towns throughout the Cosmos. We'll see if longevity cancels death!

Land life is reduced, but sea life flourishes. Coral reefs and floating algae islands multiply. Mother-Sea transforms surviving into thriving. Ma opens her star-filled bosom to us, providing a path thru countless wormhole OrmNet Portals.

Atlanta *tea-sippers* never imagined seven Atlanta hills as tropical islands. No one predicted a 1,000 years at Atlanta's sea-shore. Kids call it a *1,000 year picnic.* They read Ray Bradbury's *The Million Year Picnic,* in ancient pre-Cataclysm *The Martian Chronicles*.

Is Ma's survival plan nine gals to one guy? It's the *new normal* for people and most critters. Changes in land fauna seem more like adaptation than evolution. *Island dwarfism* seems likely. Critters lose mass as land habitats warm, shrink, and are isolated.

Cataclysms tend to shrink land species, numbers, and body mass. Dinosaurs cleared the way for birds and small critters. Ice-age mammoths left the Earth to small mammals. The Cat brought a warm global sea, and a vast reduction in land life.

Recently, in the Cosmic Matriarch Diary, Atlanta pre-puberty kids found pre-Cataclysm archives describing an early cataclysm on Earth. Back 1.7 billion years, the First Mass Extinction Event set evolution for aerobic oxygen using bacteria, likely Cyanobacteria.

A 2022 report from West Africa of 17 *natural nuclear events* were traced back 1.7 billion years. U-235/U-238 remain with decay products Neodymium (Nd-143) and Ruthenium (Ru-99). These are dated to a stellar event six billion years before the origin of Earth.
The point is that kids dig up some fascinating stuff. Uranium radiation decay suggests a prior supernova event. That event possibly formed the Solar System and Earth. This further supports our belief in *perpetual cosmic energy recycling*.

*

Matriarchs *meet peoples' needs and contribute as they are able.* Ma consists of all cosmic energy, endlessly recycling. Ma is living conscious energy in the infinite present. All energy as Mother-Cosmos is Cosmology theory as well as a matriarch belief system.

Ma is Mother-Nature and Mother-Cosmos. Everything flows from Ma's infinite perpetually recycling and transforming energy. We share Ma's cosmic mind and thoughts. Ma gives cosmic consciousness to complex critters such as people.

Matriarchs do as they've always done: surviving, nurturing, and caring for people and all life. We extend families and tunnel-towns throughout the Cosmos. We are cosmic stewards of life. Kids call us *cosmic stick insects*, *cosmic park rangers*. That's fine!

We get many cute and amusing names. And it's OK! As Elder stewards, we encourage laughter as a vital health factor. Often, we're the brunt of the jokes. And that's perfect. It shows that kids are actively thinking and exploring all possibilities.

People are replaced only as they leave the Earth. Most kids leave thru wormhole OrmNets, as off-earth interns. But first kids must complete puberty and contribute eggs-sperm to seed-banks. Turnover makes parent-team birth the constant challenge we need.

Ten-million on Earth and ten-thousand in each off-earth world are the limits that encourage new nests in new worlds. As over-population led to Earths' last Cataclysm, *nine-to-one* gals-to-guys is seen as vital to well-being on Earth and in the Cosmos.

Over the millennium we lose body mass, growing tall and slim. With large oval heads and lighter bodies, we resemble the praying mantis. Brain, heart, lungs, and circulation expand, as lower body mass shrinks, especially digestive and genital organs are reduced.

Since the Cat, *in-body* gestation became a deadly option. Birth canals atrophy. All births are now external, *in vitro*. Mothers' uterus

tissue is cultured to line incubators. Seed bank embryos are cultured as fetus and infant develop in uterus tissue incubators.
Hormone balance is kept with virus-phage as monitors. Gone are violence, aggression, greed, suffering and tyranny. Optimum hormones, such as oxytocin, estrogen, and progesterone support nurturing. Pre-Cataclysm abuse is now Mutterrecht nurturing.

Hormone moderation significantly improves emotional intelligence. As with Greening, hormonal and biochemical optimized balance supports longevity. Body balance with optimum immunity are maintained by virus-phage micro-bots.

With patriarchy, birth mortality-morbidity were common. Mutterrecht (MR) ended birth mortality-morbidity. MR ended the threats of over-population, pollution, and patriarch power greed. MR is part of Ma, Deep Mother Cosmos. And Ma keeps on giving!

Incubator birth, from embryo to infant, renders birth fully viable. Zero tolerance for mortality-morbidity is the only acceptable MR option. MR advises population limits on new worlds. Except for some residual parent anxiety, birth suffering has ended.

*

Most people have *gone Green*. Chloroplast tattoos (tats) provide expanded: minds, energy, and longevity. Elders increased *Green* longevity soon after the Cataclysm. *Greening* nutrition is supplemented with plant tonics, juices, ferments, and teas.

Like Enders, a few are not yet Green or are just token green (Toks). Life choices are freely made. Some choose to be total animal (Tots), not half-ass veg-imals. Few support that view, but choice respect is a must. *Greens* also call themselves *Cosmics*.

Plants expel oxygen as a *waste* gas. Photosynth *Greens* utilize the extra oxygen to energize lungs, heart, circulation, and brain. *Greens* expel very little waste oxygen. But *Greens'* oxygen adds to Earths' oxygen, and is greatly aids breathing under Mother-Sea.

Most *Green* parent teams implant their fetus with stem cell chloroplast genes during incubation. In their first decade, *Green* kids are multiple seed donors. Most crave internships in off-world tunnel-towns. And new world exploration is a popular pursuit.

Kids leaving longhouses go mostly *walkabout* on *vision quests* or as off-earth interns. There may be a few Enders each year, tired of life and craving *new dimensions*. But natural death is becoming rare. We say that *natural death is increasingly un-natural*.

*

Two guys are in this pre-puberty training session. Guys are trained by the gals who pick them early-on as sperm donors for parent birth teams. With the onset of puberty, the egg-sperm *Gathering* begins. The Gathering starts the Deep Mother fertility rites.

Native mothers have a genetic survival advantage. This is true globally, but especially in the Montreal-Atlanta-Havana island clans. Before the Cataclysm, patriarchs took coastal areas, forcing the native people onto the poorer but higher up-lands.

Many Cat survivors are the daughters of Native mothers. Montreal-Atlanta-Havana clans include the offspring of: Iroquois, Mohawk, Sioux, Algonquin, Kiowa, Crow, Cree, Seminole, and Hatuay in Havana. Muscogee, Creek and Cherokee are in Atlanta.

Longhouses combine open platform chickees with whatever housing imagination locals desire. Building materials are mostly bamboo, rattan, palmetto, palm fronds, but not mangrove. People and the occasional storms often alter longhouse structures.

The longhouse and chickee are designed to strengthen society and are of Iroquois and Seminole origin. On Earth and in the off-earth tunnel-towns, tribal influence remains strong. Simple life solutions are said to be gifts of Ma, Deep Mother Cosmos.

Earths' twelve metro island chains, and the many tunnel-towns in other worlds, are clans within the unified cosmic matriarch family. The only political structure is the Family as *Social State*. Stewards serve as family Guides. Leaders washed away with patriarchs.

We recreate pre-Cataclysm tribal rituals, dances, and vision quests. Fertility dances honor egg-sperm seed *Gathering.* Both ritual circle dances and social dances are open to all. All are encouraged to join the circle dances and drumming. Cheetahs are often attracted.

Rites include drumming and circle dances. Kids and Elders recreate the Stomp, Green Corn, and Matron dances. The old Veterans' dance is now Ma's Deep Mother dance. Ghost, Sun, and line dances are now Vision Quest and Spirit-walk circle dances.

Swart, the old Seminole *Black drink* like coffee provides energy, longevity, and awareness. Roasted and boiled Yaupon Holly leaves provide theobromine, caffeine, and most vital of all, the *ursolic* acid. Ursolic acid is found in apples and most fruit peels.

Kids use OrmNet wormholes for walkabout and to pursue vision quests. They seek Ma, the Deep Mother, in the challenge of new worlds. Many are inspired by OrmNet vision quests. For some it's just a lark. OrmNet drones probe for new worlds before nesting.

*

Hesta, the fifth planet orbiting the Regulus quad-stars, is in the Constellation Leo of the Milky Way Galaxy. Hesta tunnel-towns were first nested over 500 years ago. Marya, Freya, and Sophia, in the Andromeda Galaxy, were nested just three centuries back.

Lately, popular internships are in the tunnel-towns of planets Hesta, Marya, Freya and Sophia. Hesta Cloud beings stimulate sensory imagination. Marya, Freya, and Sophia plasma electron beings provide direct gene insights, much like Visitors on Earth.

Hesta Cloud beings resemble Cyanobacteria clouds on Earth. Plasmas are sentient electron energy beings. *Plasma electrons* are the most common form of cosmic matter. Plasmas are far more prevalent than carbon-based beings, such as Cyano and People.

Plasma energy on Earth forms lightning and much free electrical discharge. Plasma is *electron loss.* Energy renewal for cellular life requires *electron transfer.* Electron transfer is both electron loss and gain. *Flux re-balance* energy provides a net electron gain.

Electron energy, for all cells and plasmas, needs some form of electron transfer. Plasma beings consisting of electrons are in constant flux. Plasma and human survival depend on electrons in constant motion. And life energy depends on electro-magnetism.

Matriarchs say that *electrons* are part of Deep Mother. This makes sense since electrons unite all matter, from plasma to Cyanobacteria to people. If true, then Ma, Deep Mother provides the electro-magnetic energy mass for this universe.

On Marya, Freya, and Sophia, sentient plasma electrons are invited into one's mind. Plasma may provide genetic and cellular code or provide hosts with requested data, code and information. But it is as energy transfer electrons that plasmas mainly function.
Researchers suggest that plasma electrons energize our mind. Since electron transfer is the common energy source, this is as reasonable an origin as any other. The Cosmic Matriarch Diary suggests electrons and Cyano are synergistic in creating people.

The human body is a busy place. Of our trillions of body cells, more than half are a vast spectrum of microbes. Cyano may have started *body-building* people, but countless other beings contribute to this complex human critter. At our core we are all electrons.

Perhaps the key plasma message is: *Ma, Mother Cosmos is infinite living energy code, endlessly recycling and transforming energy. Consciousness is the core of cosmic energy, and all beings. Reality consists of our awareness and experience of this instant.*

As trainer for pre-puberty kids, they must know that they are never alone. That's the point of this *togetherness* stuff. With countless electrons, microbes and cells, we're vastly more than a sum of our parts. Yet we're also *ourselves*. Yes kids, we are truly never alone!

*

Since the Cataclysm, we code countless Nanobot drones (Nbots) to search for suitable tunnel-town worlds. Nbots provide links to off-earth nests such as those in Hesta, Marya, Freya, and Sophia. Nbots test OrmNet wormhole domains for transfer viability.

Nbot code is constantly revised. First level search is for Sun-like orange or red dwarf stars. Second level is for rocky electro-magnetic worlds. Third level is for temperate-water-oxygen planets. But *Lifeless* worlds are seeded with Cyanobacteria spoors.

On Earth, energy collecting Dyson Rings are made largely from space and satellite debris. Drone scavengers supply debris to orbiting drone automatories. Cosmic regions with non-human Dyson-like devices may be mapped but are carefully avoided.

Dyson energy is collected from nearby stars and Cosmic Microwave Background radiation. Dysons now collect Cosmic-, Gamma-, and X-radiation. Laser-pulse plasma energy packets are transmitted to satellite Batacitor storage until needed.

Matriarch metros and tunnel-towns that are on- and off-Earth share: Dysons, magnetic monopoles, GravLevs, wormholes, fusion, and all tech. It's agreed not to use wastful and polluting rocket propulsion. Laser fusion is reserved for tunneling.

*

Twelve Earth metros share in salvaging obsidian tablets from under sea libraries. These are gathered from Sphinx, Vatican, BritMuse, Louvre, Congress, Alexandrian, and other great ancient libraries in Mother-Sea. We hunger for and share all knowledge.

All are encouraged to use Archive InterLingua (AIL). Mother-Sea tablets are added to the cosmic AIL WebNet. Tablet translation enjoys cosmic popularity. Kids and elders are especially adept at deciphering obsidians, paleolithic glyphs, and cuneiform tablets.

AIL provides translation code for hundred's of ancient languages. Those who crave puzzels and mysteries love tablet translation. Translated tablets are posted for coments on the Cosmic Matriarch Diary. AIL ciphers are a major source of recreation and learning.

Soon after the Cataclysm, *MaSprek* grew rapidly mostly from English, German, Spanish, and French. The MaSprek Cosmic Lexicon grows daily, and is documented in the Cosmic Matriarch Diary. All translated tablets are published in MaSprek.

We form *Spreks* language study groups. Included are: Basque, Keltic, Catalan, Iroquois, Spanglish, and Nordish. Most all pre-Cataclysm Spreks are available for study on many networks and web links. Spreks are mostly learned via *ShlafKen* sleep learning.

*

On an open chickee platform, twelve kids sit on palm mats in a circle. Bamboo, sand-oaks and empress palms sway in the sea breeze. Kids rebuilt the chickee six months ago, after the last storm collapse. Storm building is part of pre-puberty training.

Another group of kids will rebuild the chickee after the next storm collapse. They meditate in the sea breeze. Repeating the mantra: *Ohm ... Shakti ... Kahli ... Ma*. Gulls dive for crabs scampering into the mangrove, as the house-cat size dwarf cheetahs chase them.

What remains of seasons are the periodic typhoons every four to six months. With satellite storm warning, most retreat into tunnel-towns. Living, recreation and tech facilities extend thru miles of tunnel, along with duplicates of all surface plant and animal life.

The kids are part of the Marya longhouse puberty training team. Most longhouses have training classes. On reaching puberty most kids plan off-earth internships. At puberty, kids will go on wormhole OrmNet vision quests, to celebrate their seed-banking.

Fertility rites begin as egg-sperm seed donors are added to the parent list. Puberty training kids learn life skills, including seed-banking, embryo-cell culture, incubator birthing, and related parenting skills. Kids form parent teams when listed for birthing.

After seed-banking, years may pass before donors are called to form birth parent teams. It depends on the need for more people.

Replacement is geared to Earth's ten-million *carrying capacity*. Globally, thousands of kids intern to off-earth worlds each year.

Pala, the Marya longhouse steward, signals the kids to follow her in Prana-yama. A few minutes later Pala asks: "At our last session I asked y'all to read Perrault's *Cinderella* story from the late 17th Century. Why read this ancient story, who can say?"

Hildi: "*Cinderella* lays bare the not so hidden nature of patriarch abuse. The story is fairly simple, having a certain charm as a patriarch morality tale. *Cinderella* provides a narrow view of a tyrannical patriarch world that's hard to understand these days."

Isis: "*Cinderella* reveals the suffering of women under patriarchy. Reading *Cinderella* and other folk tales, it's strange that gals usually remained home while guys often left home *to seek their fortune*. Why was that? But the fairy-godmother seems familier."

Pala: "*Cinderella* reveals both subtle and obvious patriarch family abuse. Cindi lives with the common abuse of women and children. The fairy-godmother may be an appearance of Ma, Deep Mother. But what does *Cinderella* say about family, anyone?"

Bern: "The fragmented nuclear family was forced to serve patriarchs. The father in these stories is often an absentee merchant. Merchant-fathers strived to gain wealth, resources and power to enrich themselves. Aid to family was often secondary."

Lil: "The *Cinderella* family is part of patriarch slave society. There was only a pretense of family sharing, and only a feeble attempt to meet human needs. The step-mother enforced social class, forcing Cinderella to labor to extremes for the step-family women."
Dea: "For *Cinderella* the family was a prison. The step-family were prison guards, and task-masters. Constricted step-families resulted from the patriarch break-up of matriarch clan and tribe. Abused and fragmented clans became *nuclear* families."

Pala: "Excellent insight, y'all. The story suggests that when her mother was alive *Cinderella* was loved and valued. This portrayal of the patriarch family is bleak, but far from the worst. Many dark tormenting *folk- fairy tales* were written by the Brothers Grimm.

"The fairy-godmother, I suggest, is Ma, Deep Mother, a remnant of the Great Goddess or Cosmic Mother. Here's an excerpt of the Great Goddess Isis that's almost 3,000 years old. Isis later becomes the wish-granting fairy-godmother, who brings hope as follows:

This quotation is from an early Latin novel: The *Golden Ass*, by Lucius Apuleius. This ancient Roman writer invokes Isis and she replies as we might expect a Deep Cosmic Mother to reply:

I am she that is the natural mother of all things,
Mistress governess of all elements, the initial progeny of worlds,
Chief of the powers divine,
Queen of all that are in Hell (underworld),
Principal of them all that dwell in Heaven,
Manifested alone and under one form of all gods and goddesses....

"Notice, that gals stayed home while guys 'l*eft home to seek their fortune.*' That's important as ancient matriarch tribes sent surplus sons to complete neighbor clans and tribes. Women managed tribal resources and reproduction long before the patriarch era.

"The North American Iroquois Federation exemplified matriarch tribal stewardship. Tribal matrons appointed and deposed chiefs. Matrons controlled tribal resources and decided on supporting or withholding support for war parties and punitive actions.

"Cinderella's *absentee* father suggests a fragmented *nuclear* family. Patriarch *property* included women, children, household, land, nature, and clan resources. Violence, abuse and theft degrade nature into property. But matriarch nurture restores Mutterrecht."

Lal: "Victimization is painfully detailed in the *Hansel and Gretel* story. Grimm folk tales are full of cruelty, mostly patriarch inspired.

Many of these tales portrays patriarch marriage much like slavery. Patriarch myth blamed women for their own victimization.

*

Pala: "Longhouses strengthen family and free us from the bondage of marriage. Mutterrecht (MR) is the only law people have and need. MR nurtures life, flowing from the depth of Ma, Mother-Cosmos. MR is cosmic energy recycling for complex critters.

"Without intending to, most folk tales deal with patriarch abuse. Hundreds of so-called Household-, Old Wives-, Fairy-, and Folk-Tales were collected. As with bibles, these tales were ancient matriarch tales, corrupted to serve patriarch mythology.

"Grimm Brothers provide an elaborate chronicle of patriarch abuse. Not that it was their intention to condemn patriarchs, or maybe it was. But Grimm tales provide a torturous account of patriarch tyranny. As a child, the Grimm tales made me fearful.

"Before the Cataclysm, Grimm tales were considered charming children's morality tales. Most tales involve greed, violence, as well as the victimization of women and children. Tales of Hans Christian Andersen are much gentler than the Grimm stories.

"Before the Cataclysm, I studied Political Economy, analyzing global violence, exploitation, especially the patriarch war against women, children, and nature. But that was long before the Cataclysm. By reducing humanity the Cataclysm humanized it.

"Matriarchs nurture *Tolerant symbiotes (*Tsyms*)* life. Most of life are Tsyms. But patriarchs were often *parasitic.* A nurturing Mother Goddess was violently replaced with a rapacious Father God. Matriarchs restore Ma, Deep Mother-Nature, Mother-Cosmos.

"Ma was the cosmic recycler-transformer long before, and after patriarchs were sufficiently numerous to force their tyranny. Ma is perpetual life, code, and energy—Deep Mother. She is cosmic energy. Ma transforms recycles cosmic energy thru all mothers.

"Before the Cataclysm, most men were nurturing and caring, as they are now. But the tyranny of relatively few sociopath oligarchs overwhelmed the Earth. How does the matriarch family differ from the patriarch family? Any thoughts about this?"
Teri: "Matriarch families share duties and resources. Needs are met with available resources. But mostly people need attention, love, nurture and care, which is a major part of meeting human needs. Our material needs have greatly diminished over the millennium."

Tya: "Kids are a vital part of cosmic energy recycling, as are Elders, stewards and all people. No one is any more or less important than anyone else. As energy is everywhere it is easily shared. And all gals and guys are mothers' children."

Pala: "Excellent, we all learn from Ma. Mother cats care for their kits, as kits learn to hunt. Cats, especially cheetahs, and people have evolved together. What could we learn from cats by watching them hunt? Watch cheetahs hunt to see what you can learn.

"For our next session here's a challenge: If life adapts to stress, how does a millennium of adaptation change *Homo sapiens* into *Gyna cosmos sapiens*? Divide into teams of four. Each team to provide a surprise media to respond to this challenge."

*

Pala and the twelve kids grab flying suits from under the chickee, and go to the shore. Little cheetah kits wrap around their ankles, craving attention. Kids run laughing, chased by the kits. Toma the smallest of the kids, not yet six feet, sings out loudly:

"Scat cat, catch a rat.
Catch a rat and you'll be fat.
She caught a rat and now she's fat."

All hug Toma, singing along. Pala joins in, laughing thru her tears.

They run toward the waves and into the wind. Flapping their gull-like *Graphel* wings, sea breezes easily lift them into the air. Pala follows some gulls as they fly into the wind. Kids follow Pala and the gulls into the wind and over the coral reefs.

As crabs run from the incoming surf, gulls dive for them. Cheetah kits race for the scampering crabs, catching some ahead of the gulls. Gulls shrieking at their loss, begin diving and pecking at the kits. With their long claws some racing kits catch gulls in flight.

The kids chase the gulls. Cheetah kits run into the mangrove dragging crabs and gulls in their mouths. Two kits, bleeding from attacking gulls, race into the waves to salve their wounds. It's unusual for cheetahs and gulls to attack each other, unless stressed.

Following in the wake of the gulls, first Pala, then the kids look like the bows on a kite tail. Stressed gulls shriek loudly. Pala leads the flight of kids to circle the coral reefs, then back to the shore. Removing flying gear, they all stroll slowly back to the longhouse.

Pala asks them to sip fruit juices and rest in the longhouse atrium shade. The kids are too excited to rest or even sit still. They gab about cheetahs, crabs, and seagulls. They've already begun talking about parenting teams, as well as seed-banking.

Toma: “Before the Cataclysm patriarchs were the top predators. Now it’s cheetahs. Do cats hunt any other critters besides crabs?”

Lee: “I see them hunt mice and squirrels. They drag them into the kudzu. When I tried to stop a kill, cheetahs hissed *scat*. They voice words clearly when angry. We've all heard them.”

Pala: “They fish from the coral reefs and swallow small fish. Sensing sand sharks they race for shore. Cheetahs can do a furious underwater paddle, when threatened. Before the Cataclysm, cats were not great swimmers or fond of water, except with fish in it.”

Dea: “Cheetahs also eat kudzu, or at least nibble on it. I see them nibble on the thick blades of buffalo grass and other tender greens. It’s for the veg juices, I think. Greens help them cough-up hair balls. Do ya think cheetahs will ever live on sunlight like us?”

*

A couple of nine-year-olds plan to apply as interns to the tunnel-town on planet Freya, in the Andromeda galaxy. With Pala's help, they learn *Garda*, a viral phage technology code. Garda phage virus selectively adapt to protect and enhance cells.

Pala: "Glad y'all are interested in bacteria-phage. Garda phage monitor cells to reduce stress. Garda are *heuristic*, that is they learn by saving code packets from previous challenges. They're also transgenic, providing horizontal gene transfer, when coded.

"As y'all learn coding, study Garda phage code. Segregating harmful code, Garda phage add mal-code to their genetic database, in preparation for related threats. Our words *goddess* and *guard* are from the ancient Celtic *Garda,* meaning to secure and protect."

Jera: "At first we wanted to learn Cyanobacteria tech. Checking the coms convinced us that Cyano tech is too damn popular. But Garda phage code has more intern openings, more of a mystery. That's really what's so attractive. We all just love mystery.

"Learning Garda code is our goal. Planet Freya coms indicate a shortage of interns in this field. Much of the work so far is based on Nanobot tech. Learning Nanobot planet-search coding is a start. It's like the way Garda phage *search and protect* cells."

Pala: "Sounds like a plan is shaping-up, glad to help! But Garda phage code is more complex than Nanobot. Besides phage code, y'all need to learn CRISPR miRNA and DNA/RNA transduction code upgrades. It involves protein synthesis and supression coding.

"It's all code: Phage, Garda, virus, people, life, energy and the Cosmos. Fractal code geometry provides the *scaffolding* for life energy. We're all energy code packages. Pre-Cataclysm, I was a code instructor, among other roles. Code is far more complex now.

"Phage virus tech pre-dates the Cataclysm by at least 100 years. Bacteria-phage were first found in local waters to treat antibiotic resistant infections. Phage are specific for limited classes of microbes. Most phage are synergistic with select microbes.

“Not only are phage unique for bacteria species, but also for the infections being treated. Phage naturally overcome antibiotic resistance. Specific phage therapy can be cultured in a few hours. Phage were first used to vaccinate and to adapt Greening genes.

“Phage databases exist for all antibiotic resistant bacteria. A millennium later, phage mostly deliver gene modification. Phage can strengthen cells. Potentiated sulfonamide phage now enhance immunity, as needed. Sulfa-adapted phage are especially versatile.

“Phage, in addition to T-cells, guard our body in advance of potential problems. These are the Garda phage that insert longevity factors into our cells. Increasingly, selective miRNA, mitochondria, and greening chloroplasts are delivered via phage.

“In addition, Garda support overall biochemical regulation. Garda phage insert photosynth chloroplasts into skin cells, as skin patch vax tattoos. Phage *learn* from host cells, preventing harmful cell cancers. Along with Cyano, Phage are part of Ma's *health package*.

“Y’all provide a vital addition to longevity by interning in Garda phage coding. I suggest y’all learn the ancient Internet: virus code, protocols, drivers, and robotic network crawler bots. Y’all know that kids learn a lot easier than Elders. That’s an added incentive.

“The next challenge is: What type of code was involved in the shift from matriarchy to patriarchy. Hint: Likely, it began at the end of the last ice age and Great Flood cataclysm about 15,000 years ago. Let’s see what y’all find the next time we get together.”

Lil: “How could patriarchs fabricate beliefs in father-gods? Didn’t they realize that all people come from their mothers, and her mother came from her mothers, *und so weiter*, back to the one and only Ma, Deep Mother, Mother-Cosmos, Mother-Nature.

“This was found in an ancient pre-Cataclysm book on myths, by Joseph Campbell, recognizing the primal role of the Great Mother:

As the infant is linked to its mother in a profound participation mystique, even to such a degree that it will absorb, and thus inherit, her tensions and anxieties, so has mankind been linked to the moods and weathers of its mother Earth. This quote is from:

HISTORICAL ATLAS OF WORLD MYTHOLOGY VOL I: THE WAY OF THE ANIMAL POWERS PART I: MYTHOLOGIES OF PRIMITIVE HUNTERS AND GATHERERS, page 47. Harper and Rowe, 1988."

Pala: "Lil, I've been around over 1,000 years and I still ask myself that question. How could patriarchs have believed as they did? And how could they live with over 6,000 years of atrocities. The only answer I come up with is that it was not the vast majority of guys.

"Out-of-control malignantly aggressive psychopaths were the problem. Like Genghis Khan, Hitler, Stalin, and assorted global oligarchs, it was a small number of patriarchs that destroyed Mother-Earth. Ancient archives will list these human malignancies.

"Millions of people struggled to save the Earth. But the few toxic leaders continued what must have been for them compulsion, even into the Cataclysm. Archives show why only the Cataclysm could provide a fresh start. All the reforms and revolutions did little.

"The illusion of *meaningful reform* certainly motivated many millions of sincere and dedicated people. Some were in fact the wealthiest people on Earth. But a relatively few globally malignant oligarchs repeatedly trashed all efforts at benefiting the Earth.

"With this perspective, it may be seen that a *higher-power* was needed to save the Earth. This is where Ma, Mother-Nature, Mother-Cosmos, Deep Cosmic-Mother, or perhaps some other cosmic conscious being was forced to provide the Cataclysm.

"It matters little how we see Ma. I may envision Ma as the Divine Cosmic Mother. Sometimes I think of Ma as the Great Cosmic

Goddess. Her only task is to recycle and transform cosmic energy. Ma may only be capable of correcting cosmic energy imbalance.

"Does Ma's cosmic work seem dull, repetitive? So as not to fixate on her cosmic work, possibly Ma leaves all the thinking and consciousness to the more complex critters, such as people, plasma electrons, and the many complex beings who are as yet unknown.

"While in an expansive and speculative mood, I ask y'all to imagine the perception and consciousness of all complex cosmic beings who comprise Ma's cosmic mind. Perhaps cosmic wormholes unify the totality of Ma's cosmic mind.

"Is the human mind a copy, a lesser version of Ma's mind, or an integral micro in the cosmic mind? Hopefully, there will always be more questions than answers, and more mysteries than solutions. And there are certainly possibilities not yet even imagined."

*

A sudden vision flashes in my minds' eye. It's 1946. I'm a ten-year old guy. The Cataclysm is 90 years away. On Sundays, dad drives ma, my sister, and me first to his sister Rose. Cousin Bob is the same age as me. He teaches me to ride a two-wheeler bike.

The same evening dad drives us to ma's sister Laura. I enjoy both visits. We do this most Sundays in dad's 1938 black Pontiac. The aunts and uncles share much attention and love. These are happy times for all of us. My aunts are like supporting mothers.
The vision continues, it's 1949. Dad got me a used English racer bike. Carelessly, I ride my bike into heavy Miami Beach 42nd Street traffic. It's near where we live. I crash the bike into a slow-moving car. Dad's food market is across the street, within view of my folly.

The front wheel is badly bent. I'm not badly hurt. The car driver attempts to help me but in my confused panic I rush away from scene. I fear that dad will see the accident from his market. That night dad notices the bike. I say I smashed the wheel into a tree.

A week later, I buy a friend's heavy old bike with a large basket for seven dollars. The friend's family is moving out of state. The bike also comes with a paper route for the Miami Beach Sun. After school, delivering the evening Sun, I earn $5 to $8 a week.

In the summer of 1950 the Nautilus Middle School nears completion. I travel all over Miami Beach with my bike. And I'm into all sorts of adventures. Exploring the Nautilus school building site, I step on a nail. It goes thru my sneaker sole and into my foot.

With cool resolve, I ride my bike to dad's market and tell him what happened. Dad drives me to emergency for antibiotic and tetanus shots. Dad is pleasant and understanding about my accident. I'm impressed with dad's repeated kindness, in spite of my antics.

Weeks later I start the term at Nautilus Middle School. I'm in awe of Mr. Platt's math class. It's my first encounter with basic geometry, metrics, measures, climate math, logs, and exponents. Mr. Platt tells amazing war stories of his time as a B-29 gunner.

DOUBLE GANGERS

Can deep imagining of Schrödinger's cat access parallel worlds or dimensions? That the cat is both dead and alive depends on imagining the cat in multiple places simultaneously. This thought experiment needs deep imagination.

Imagining Schrödinger's cat has me wondering if passing college Physics would have changed my life, long before the Cataclysm. I was on the high school honor role, even with A's in Physics. But in high school my attention was on academics, with few distractions.

It's hard to admit to myself: *I failed college Physics twice*. Physics theory has always been clear to me. But solving Physics math problems continues to escape me. Even with mastering Calculus theory, the math still escape me.

Deep Mem (DM) permits reliving past life events, in detail. With DM we can return to problem events, often for resolution. DM allows sorting thru our memory banks and targeting the *mems* to add or eliminate. DM requires careful evaluation and planning.

Thoughts, images, sensations, and emotions can be reclaimed from deep *mems*. But the linkage of reclaimed *mems* can injure the mem banks. My dad's passing, along with college and fraternity demands, intensified my angst and distracted me from academics.

Likely, workbooks with the relevant Physics problems could have been found and mastered. This I did not do. Now Physics math can be implanted by viral micro-needle, or even as nasal spray vaccine. At the time, I wanted medical school acceptance, not completion.

I received a letter of acceptance for first year University of Miami Medical School. But I needed to pass Physics to begin. That was a story I told myself. A second Physics failure was my escape from what I imagined to be an intolerable medical school burden.

Looking back over 1,000 years, I view medical school as a slid down the *razor-blade* of life. It still cuts into my psyche. Removing the medical school pursuit mem was my final decision. Targeted plasma electron pulse effectively removed that mem.

Plasma Pulsing (PP) electrons provide deep imagining. Giving direct access from perception to genetic data access. Brain energy electrons allow instant evaluation of past experience mems, such as Physics exams, medical careers, and even Schrödinger's cats.

PP electrons are micro *Visitors*, as are the trillions of microbes that create people. As Visitors, PP electrons enliven electro-magnetic life. Electrons and countless other microbial visitors help transform people from Earth-bound beings into Cosmos-directed beings.

Plasma electrons help create people and all life. Electrons initiate, lend, and activate mind-body energy. That lightning and electrons provide a cosmic *spark of life* seems quite likely. Life seems to be electro-magnetic and dependent on electron transfer.

Trillions of micro energy beings make us who we are. These beings are everywhere providing electron energy. But life forms perpetually change. That can explain why people are transforming from *Homo sapiens sapiens* to *Gyna cosmos sapiens.*

Just as the cosmic energy *scaffold* keeps changing, so too do all forms of life energy change. Cosmos is compared to a hat with infinite possibilities. All possibilities are pulled from the hat, into reality. Eventually, horses and people must exist, and repeatedly.

No matter how many possibilities Deep Mother pulls from her hat, there's an infinite number remaining. Housecat-size cheetahs would evolve eventually, in various places, and repeatedly. Microbes live on many worlds, but more complex life is elusive.

Cosmic energy is such that infinite possibilities, worlds, universes, realities, and dimensions may be imagined. Schrödinger's cat is infinitely *alive and not alive*. Cosmic possibilities include cats and people that are both alive and not alive. Double gangers live!

*

Kids meet in the Isis longhouse atrium. It's the final year of pre-puberty training. Lela, the Elder trainer from Earth is a close kin. Since the Cataclysm, all people nesting in the hundreds of tunnel-towns, in as many worlds, are all kin. All are one cosmic family.

Lela: "As y'all become parents, mastering birth technology is becoming more of a reality. Birth tech stewards tell me y'all are well along in embryo, fetus and infant incubator mastery. But fetal fluid metabolism and maintenance needs more work.

"As seed-bank *Gathering* aproaches, additional genetic tech skills will be needed. Y'all need to learn coding: miRNA, DNA-methylation, longevity, viral-phage, and skin chloroplast Greening. While these are largely automated, your understanding is still vital.

"To alter gene expression, regulate proteins, and modify DNA, carbon-hydrogen methyl groups (CH2) may be added or deleted from fetal target genes. These *cook-book* skills may be phage- coded. These skills may be *cook-book* but y'all need to learn them.

"We need to discuss Deep Mother and Consciousness. We call her Mother-Nature, Cosmic-Mother, Mother-Cosmos, Isis, Ma, and other names. I call her Ma for short. Activate *MindRecord* for all our sessions. Y'all will need to review and discuss all our sessions.

"In ancient Chinese traditions, people were created by the heavenly goddess NÜWA. She created humanity from yellow clay, out of her lonliness. Look in *WikiArchives* for the full story. NÜWA also repaired the chaos in heaven. Guess who caused the chaos?

"Ma forms our mind and body. She provides our consciousness *subjectively* as Mutterrecht. *Objectively*, Ma is cosmic energy. Ma is the countless microbes and electrons comprising people, plants, and all life. Ma is Deep Mother, she's the reality of cosmic energy.

"For next week, search the Mother and Goddess archives. See how many different names there are. Search *WikiArchives*. Notice that the earliest deities were caves, wells, and stone monoliths. Ma is also in the womb-like tunnels and lava tubes of all tunnel-towns.

"Ma is the totality of all cosmic energy. She is *objective* and *subjective* reality. Ma's reality is timeless, infinite and perpetual. She is the energy in every body cell. Ma is the essence of all energy. Forms may change but her energy recycles without end.

"We constantly create Ma and Ma creates us. As cosmic energy, we are endlessly recycled, recreated, and transformed. Ma is cosmic consciousness. If we are renewed and transformed, it's because Ma works Her energy into all the wonders and possibilities of life.

"Please folks, it's important that we also talk about Consciousness contrasted with the possibility that we may be living in a simulation. There are certain tell-tale signs of the *conscious* and the *simulated.* This issue was discussed long before the Cataclysm.

"As y'all search cultural patterns before the Cataclysm, notice that patriarchys pushed games and gaming to strengthen their hold on people. A vast industry arose to simulate electronic game realities. Simulations were designed to reinforce dependency on patriarchs.

"Game simulation entrapped millions. Before the Cataclysm, serious discussions spread the idea that the so-called *real-world* might be a grand simulation, or Sim. *Gaming*, as with gambling, was patriarch-toxic, exploiting and trapping people.

"Gaming became a contest between *Reals* versus *Sims*. *Reals* intended to end tyrannical leadership and their toxic world. *Sims played-on*, regardless of consequences. *Sims* took electronic refuge, *hiding-out* in a simulated play-world dimension.

"Short term refuge in a simulated world can be therapeutic. When searching the archives, immersing in a HoloVid, drama, game, or any entertainment, it becomes a sim-world. But parent team activities create a beneficial sim-world.

"Before the Cataclysm, living conditions on Earth became increasingly intolerable, causing extreme anxiety. Patriarch leaders became increasingly violent. Testosterone toxicity only partly explains the East-West war and Pandemic, before the Cataclysm.

"Sky-shield satellites and orbiting nukes, designed to protect Earth from asteroids, accidentally rained down on the Earth. The resulting decade of Cataclysm tsunamis were a merciful alternative to the nuclear war about to be unleashed.

"What remains from those anxious times is the question: Are we living a reality or simulation? And does it matter? Have any of you checked archives on this question, of living in Reality versus Simulation? Some say that the reality we create becomes our sim."

Lil: "We study social-cultural conditions that led to the Cataclysm. As you suggest, gaming was a sim retreat from a painful reality. Initially, a global viral pandemic led to health-mandated *social-distancing,* and a retreat into electronic gaming, the Sims."

Jan: "Global Internet videos encouraged a retreat into an electronic sim reality. The global corporate entertainment, media and consumer industry provided a simulated reality. It was at an ever higher cost, eventually enslaving a users' mind, and life support.
"Before the East-West war broke-out, a book was published early in 2022. It summarized reality-simulation issues: *REALITY+ virtual worlds and the problems of philosophy*, by David J. Chalmers. Sim reality was a retreat from a painful world."

Pala: "Pre-Cataclysm com media played on people's fear. It was about consuming, greed, wealth and power. Public com media increased patriarch wealth and power. It's hard to understand since Mutterrecht long ago removed the cause of most of our fears.

"Patriarchs were both the cause and effect of pre-Cataclysm fears. Over-population is the cause I have in mind. And patriarch power-greed fed the global cancer: by metastasizing people. Patriarchs gave the Earth 6,000 years of violence, war, pestilence, and fear.

"The two benefits that people crave most in life are *meaning* and *security*. Ma, Deep Mother, Matriarchs, Mutterrecht, and Mother-

Cosmos continue to give us meaning and security over the last 1,000 years. But to a large extent we must credit the Cataclysm.

"The population plague was unlikely to be cured, even with the most sincere human efforts. It needed the impersonal wisdom and resolve of Ma to impose a *final solution.* Ma often gives us what we need, not what we want. It's the ultimate value of cataclysms.

Isis: "That's true. Matriarch society provides meaning and security, meeting personal and family needs. Mutterrecht is a love of life, increasing nurture, caring, and kindness. Suffering, scarcity, and pain was patriarchy. Love, meaning, and security is matriarchy.

"In the Matriarch Cosmos, people and all life-energy form a dynamic ever-changing family. We're part of an energy recycling cosmic society. Over the millennium, longhouse living includes everyone. Longhouse living is a great Iroquois innovation."

Dana: "By eliminating scarcity, deprivation and fear, Mutterrecht is the only rule we need. Limiting births on Earth, encourages exploration and nesting throughout the Cosmos. We go to new worlds since Ma, Deep Mother sets a clear path for us.

"In matriarch antiquity a similar energy equilibrium was achieved. Looking back, perhaps as much as a million years, early mothers achieved what was called in ancient myth a *Golden Age*. That myth is based on the essence of a reality that we again renew.

"In WikiArchives, the ancient Greek poet Hesiod's *Works and Days* mentioned five ages. The first is an *Age of Gold.* It was an age of peace, harmony, stability, and prosperity—much like now. Plato also mentioned a *Golden Age*:

"In that *Golden Age* the Earth provided for all needs and people lived easily with nature. People lived to an old age, remaining youthful, passing peacefully from body to spirit life, living on as guardians. This is also described in the WikiArchives."

Lela: "WikiArchives notes that Astraea presided in the *Golden Age*, until the end of the *Silver Age*. But in the *Bronze Age* men became violent and greedy. Astraea fled to the stars and now appears as the Virgo Constellation, holding Libra scales of justice."

Dana: "Do you think the *Bronze Age* is the era when patriarch dominance became a tyrannical force in the world? And what of five ages? Are they ages of: Earth, Gold, Silver, Bronze, Iron?

Lela: "Adding Earth and Iron sounds right. Check WikiArchives for *Bronze Age*. And while at it, see what WikiArchives says about *testosterone*. See what other data are available on these subjects. Check Joseph Campbell and Robert Graves' *The Greek Myths*.

"We've talked about Gold, Silver, and Bronze ages. I suggest the Iron Age as the fourth age. Iron provided the weapnons for global patriarch war and violence. The fifth age may be the return of cosmic Mutterecht, suggesting our Earth origin.

"Now, if y'all are so inclined, put on your flying-suits. I'm going to do a flight inspection of the tunnel-town segments. We'll fly thru all ten-mile segments. Let's take a short rest after each mile segment. Y'all can join our flock or not, as you like.

PLASM

From 2026 to 2036 asteroids brought global tsunamis. One-in-a-thousand people and other land critters survived. The 13-month lunar year is now 1000 AC (After Cataclysm), or 3036 in the old 12-month solar calendar. Earth is now a tropical 99% water-world.

The Cataclysm renews the *Mutterrecht* age of *Light*, ending the *Dark* age of patriarchy. Ma is Deep Mother-Cosmos recycling cosmic energy. Ma recycles the electron energy of the billions who passed, and of all the critters transformed by the Cataclysm.

Ten-million now thrive on Earth, and many millions in tunnel-towns throughout the Cosmos. It's all part of cosmic energy recycling. Mutterrecht limits people to ten-million on Earth and ten-thousand in each of the many off-earth tunnel-towns.

Plasma electrons now guide our minds. And our minds can now range thru the Cosmos as plasma. Liberation from flesh and blood makes cellular bodies less meaningful. Thanks to Ma, dreams of living as disembodied spirits move towards becoming a reality.

Cosmic energy recycling nurtures people and all life. As we nest in the Cosmos, we become cosmic stewards, Ma's cosmic acolytes. Kids call us Cosmic Park Rangers. They say we look like praying mantis, stick insects. The joke is on all of us, and that's fine.

Ma helps us, and all critters, as we adapt to smaller warmer habitats. Body mass declines as height exceeds seven feet. While lower body organs shrink, upper body lungs, circulatory system, and brain grow. Thanks to Ma, we become a human comedy!

It's no joke that the human body can no longer give birth to live babes. As reproductive organs shrink, external incubator birth is our only viable option. From seed-banks to incubators, kids train as parent-teams. Kids become incubator-to-birth parents.

Living as longhouse families of 100 or so, supports Mutterrecht and people replacement, as we wormhole our way to new worlds. Starting as pre-puberty kids, we start training for puberty seeding. Donating egg-sperm to seed-banks transforms kids into adults.

*

We adapt and evolve from *Homo sapiens* to *Gyna cosmos sapiens*. Aided by plasma electrons, Cyanobacteria began the great trek to humanity billions of years ago. Now, Cyano and Plasma electrons expand our minds into organs that explore the Cosmos.

Increasingly we are plasma electron beings. And we sense our deepening electrical nature. We extend and expand our minds by means of plasma electron projection. As we wormhole to new worlds, minds reach out to other minds and to the stars.

Electrons are basic to all life. People may be a recent complex version of carbon-based electricals. As we search for new worlds, *Nanobots* are coded to search for solar systems similar to Sun and Earth. Sensibly more complex electron beings may be avoiding us.

Ma's cosmic energy recyclings and transitions seem infinite, endless. It's no surprise: electron energy adapts humanity to become plasma electron beings. Electron beings, such as people, are another probability innovation in Ma's energy recycling.

On Earth and in all the worlds people nest, we share these worlds with plasma beings such as electrons, lightning, and static charge. Energy as matter is only a small part of total cosmic energy. Yet electron plasma is the most common form of matter in the Cosmos.

One of the first lessons kids learn is the scope and depth of electro-magnetic nature. It's long been known that people are electro-magnetic beings. Our minds become increasingly plasma-electric. Minds now go back in time as easily as going forward.

Events underlying the Cataclysm are constantly re-examined. The elements leading to the massive die-off point to the *inevitability* of the twin dangers of testosterone toxicity and over-population. It seems unavoidable, given the nature of patriarch leaders.

Millions of people recognized these twin dangers. But they lacked the power to bring about a meaningful change. It required the massive blunder of patriarch leaders, along with Ma's Cataclysm, to save the Earth with a total make-over.

Patriarch leaders launched Star-shield satellites to *repel* rogue asteroids. But Star-shield *attracted* asteroids. It took Mother-Nature to give Mother-Earth a renewal. The Cataclysm provided a much needed *face-lift* for Mother-Earth.
For ten years asteroids reshaped the Earth. The 1% of land above Mother-Sea is now twelve chains of small metro islands. Earth's make-over rivals that of the Great Flood 15,000 years before. But the Cataclysm restored Mutterrecht and put an end to patriarchy.

The Cataclysm washed-away population, pollution, and patriarchs. Ma now provides nine gals to one guy, for people and most critters. We're *one-in-a-thousand* surviving and thriving over a thousand years. The Cataclysm is Ma's painful but necessary gift.

Over the millennium, as our body mass declines, our height increases. Lower body organs shrink but circulation, lungs, heart, and brain expand. People increasingly resemble praying mantis insects. It's a constant source of humor. And humor is encouraged.

Strange, before the Cataclysm the praying mantis was a much admired critter. It was widely known as a beneficial insect that devoured destructive insects. Stranger still, as we adapt and evolve to nuture life in the Cosmos, we increasingly resemble the mantis.

Land survival is a form of *Island Dwarfism*. Previous cataclysms reducing land mass reduced massive fauna, favoring smaller more intelligent critters. As climate heat increases, and land is reduced, critters isolated on islands shrink in mass and number.

Small island rodents and insects thrive. While body mass declines, people are now the largest land critters. But house-cat size cheetahs are top predators. Life in Mother-Sea thrives: sea mammals, sharks, sturgeon, octopus, algae, and corals do well.

The Cataclysm reduced land critters, especially primates. Earth's face-lift and the OrmNet wormhole web encourage cosmic nesting. Ma, Deep Mother-Cosmos, transforms *Homo sapiens* into *Gyna cosmos sapiens,* as Earth-life tunnels into many new worlds.

*

Planet Freya in the Andromeda galaxy resembles Earth. Freya and two sister worlds circle twin orange suns, both smaller than Earth's Sun. OrmNet wormholes link all people-nested worlds. Since the Cataclysm, electron beings guide our Nano-bot search for worlds.

Electricals *invited* people from planet Hestia, in our Milky Way galaxy, to three planets in the Andromeda galaxy. Freya is the first nested by people. As in all off-earth worlds, people tunnel into and under mountains for safety and to reduce host world impact.
The three Andromeda worlds were located using coded Nanobots. Nanobots are microbe-size plasma electron guided light-sails. These are the first worlds nested outside the Milky Way galaxy. Many Milky Way worlds continue to be nested.

Freya, half Earth-size, is photosynth-tropical with half the Earth gravity. It's a half mountain and half marsh-like world. Water-ways cover half the surface, but with no seas or oceans. Tunnel-town nesters slowly chart Freya, exploring with air-born GravLevs.

Freya's oxygen and carbon dioxide are a bit higher than on Earth. But easily support earth-life with minor adjustment. Freya nesters have gone Green, as with most all people. Phage virus skin tatt chloroplasts produce most of people's energy and oxygen.

Freya's plants are similar to Earth's Cretaceous period, with many pineapple-like flowering bromeliads. No mobile life larger than Earth insects are evident. But GravLev floater exploration is far from complete. Dense marsh jungle slows exploratory charting.

Of keen interest are the people-size rock-like fungoids with slow metabolism. These seem to guard cave and lava tube entrances. The're called *Oncos* as they closely resemble Earth Cyanobacteria stromatolites or oncolites. The Oncos are clearly living beings.

*

After a year of frequent visits to her kin, Lela was invited to remain as a tutor in Freya's Mari longhouse. Many Earth kids seek internships on Freya, as techs are constantly needed. As an Elder surviving the Cataclysm, Lela's experience is much valued.

With all her brilliant innovations, Lela still suffers a serious math-block. She fears her math-block may hinder the kids. After a 1,000 years of over-compensation, she's determined to end her limitation. Lela remains haunted by failing Physics courses a millennia earlier.

Imagining Schrödinger's Cat, as both living and dead, puts Lela in parallel worlds. Yet she can't imagine both passing and failing university Physics. There are still occasions when Lela lets herself agonize over physics math. But she refuses to harbor self regret.

Lela's math block is a barrier. She suffers the angst of twice failing university Physics. She fears her math block will interfere with tutoring the kids. She's determined to correct the problem. It's less the math-block and more the self regret that she fears.
Dina, the tunnel-town steward, suggests that Lela either delete her math-block, or better yet, take a viral-phage vax skull patch to implant Physics and Calculus math. Kids are in danger of negative math attitudes should she continue with her limitation.

Lela is uncomfortable with mind-alts but realizes it must be done, for the kids' sake. Never before has she hesitated to help kids when possible. Certainly, she'll do what's needed now. She can't understand why she waited this long to take the vax.

She easily grasps both Physics and Calculus *theory*. For each Physics exam, Lela agonized thru endless practice problems. But no amount of practice helped her with the actual exam problems. Now, math and most mems are easily implanted with a vax.

Since Lela fully understood physics theory, she failed physics exams twice, but just slightly short of passing. Her math solutions to test problems were consistently muddled. Her Calculus math mirrored that of Physics. She'll know math like she knows code.

Lela's Fractal Geometry Energy tutorials are on HoloVid via the Cosmic OrmNet Wormhole Network. For clearity and insight, her energy tutorials are unequaled. Without the math, Lela's lectures on Cosmic Energy Transformation Recycling are widely studied.

In the main, Lela lives joyfully with creative vision and growing cosmic consciousness. But in the math world her vision is limited. She trusts the vax mem-phage implants more than mem removal. If only these were available during her university years.

Since the Cat, Lela's insights contribute to wormhole OrmNets, Quantum String Gravity, magnetic monopoles, GravLevs, and chloroplast photosynth longevity. But her belief that math obscures energy theory is no longer convincing, even to her.

*

Lela often visits kids via OrmNets. These visits are mostly by millennium Elders born before the Cataclysm. Elders comprise half the ten-million people living on Earth. Most kids plan off-earth internships, so their families often plan OrmNet visits.

Longevity is an early achievement, beginning long before the Cataclysm. Longevity became a distinct reality after the Cataclysm removed patriarchs, pollution, and population. People refer to the Cataclysm as *The Great Cleansing* and *The Awesome Face-lift*.
Land critters seem to gain intelligence as body mass declines. House-cat size cheetahs are top island predators, and *talk* with people. Cheetahs hunt small sea fish. And felines still hunt rodents as well as the housecat-size key deer, but seldom birds.

Along with tutoring kids, Lela is invited to improve links with the plasma electron beings (Plasm). She's a natural empath, well skilled with kids and the Plasm. Plasm and people study each other, sharing human minds and sensory input.

Plasm transfer energy code for electrons and photons. Lightning discharge is a known form of electron energy code. Cell electron transfer suggests that Plasm enhance life via phage virus electron code transfer, affirming that electrons are the basis of life.

Both virus and Plasm provide electron links. Both spread the code of life. Virus transfer both genetic and electron codes. Genetic code depends on electron energy transfer by means of virus in the chemical molecules that comprise genes and organic cells.

Electron-photon Plasm metabolism suggests a key form of cosmic energy recycling. Life seems to depend on electron, virus, and microbial energy transfer. Kids are asked to search: Can any form of life or energy exist without electron transfer?

Lela created the first coherent electron coding with Plasm beings. Waveform coding links neuron microtubule vibrations with electrical phase shift. Can Plasm electrons link wormholes to access diverse dimensions and universes? Now there's a challenge!

Electro-magnetic force (emf) is the result of photon and electron interaction. Emf occurs as *Fields* or *Strings* of electron waveform vibration. Electrons link neuron microtubules for sense perception and consciousness. All life forms seem to be based on emf energy.

People transform *subjective* sensory perception into *objective* experiences. Can Plasm electrons aid in bridging dimensions and universes? Waveform vibration frequencies may be involved. Plasm electrons may utilize neutrino as well as electron energy.

Transfer between dimensions may take place in dreams. Dream travel is achieved by some lucid dreamers. Many lucid dreamers record their dreams in the Cosmic Matriarch Diary. Slow *delta* brain waves are Plasm electron contact points for lucid dreaming.
Cosmic electrons suggest possible links between dimensions and universes. Plasm electrons may form brain frequencies below ELF, Extremely Low Frequencies. These may effect transfers between dimensions and universes. Then again maybe not.

Plasm may provide for Directed Lucid Dreaming, and possibly dimensional mind travel. Wormhole access fires the imagination. Research continues in quantum magnetics and *String* vibration wavefront fields. M*ore research is needed and always will be!*

Before the Cataclysm, it was suggested that the intensity of perceptual consciousness makes our experience real. Links between an experience and consciousness of it may require lucid imagination, intense sensory awareness, and deep memory.

Tactile imagining provides the experience of multiple dimensions and universes. It's another approach Lela consciously pursues with mind resident Plasm electrons. They communicate via electron frequency wave code. *All experiences are mental creations*.

Plasm beings provide electron energy throughout the Cosmos, at least in worlds with tunnel-towns. Conscious links with Plasm is evident with Visitors. Visitors directly link our mind to our DNA. Perhaps our genes are a subset of cosmic database code.

Visitors are with us at least 1,000 years, since Cataclysm, and probably long before. Visitors allow conscious gene searching. We ask ourselves if electron transfer energy is the basis of life. The positive Visitor reply is: *That cat will hunt. Keep searching!*

We ask if Dark-stuff (dark energy-matter) is a type of electro-magnetic energy. A negative Visitor reply is: *That cat won't hunt. Keep searching!* It started us searching: if Dark-stuff is actually energy. Rather, Dark-stuff may be the scaffold containing energy.

Asking if Dark-stuff is a *non-mass* geometric scaffold or substrate for mass energy, gets the positive Visitor reply: *That cat will hunt. Keep searching!* The reply invites comparison with Einstein's description of gravity as *space-time curvature geometry*.

Visitors point us in productive directions for further research. Definitive specific replies are never provided. Visitors' sense of humor, *that cat will or won't hunt,* reflects our own. It's as if Visitors are intent on challenging, rather than satisfying us.
Stewards ask that we enter Visitor questions and replies in the Cosmic Matriarch Diary (CMD). And mostly we do, except when there's too much repetition. As far as we know, Visitors have never misled us with their replies. Many similar replies are in the CMD.

Cosmic nesting is aided by Visitors. They're often called Electron Angels, or *Angels of our better nature*. Visitors do not provide easy answers for Elders or kids. And that's a good thing. The point of these discussions is to get people thinking and searching.

*

Plasm provide electron energy for nerve and brain neuron activity. They also provide electrons for all body cell energy transfers, especially of the most common cellular ADP↔ATP. Initially via lightning, Plasm electrons transform ions into living cells.

After the Cataclysm, wormhole travel began with Plasm electron energy code. Electron fields with magnetic monopoles sustain OrmNet traversable wormholes and power GravLev floaters. Plasm energy fuels human nesting throughout the Cosmos.

OrmNets permit limited access to the Cosmos. But lucid imagining may provide unlimited cosmic access. Does carbon cell electro-magnetic energy link organic to inorganic Plasm electro-magnetic energy? Visitors suggest this is the case.

Photon-electrons energize organic cells. Photon-electron Light and Dark energy sustain this universe, but perhaps not all universes. Has anyone imagined a form of energy that's independent of electro-magnetism, photons, and electrons? I keep asking this!

Both living carbon-based cells and Plasm electrons are energized by individual photons and electrons. While hydrogen is the most plentiful element in the Cosmos, plasma electricity is the most plentiful form of *mass* energy.

On the many worlds explored and nested so far, the life forms observed could easily exist on Earth. Cyano-like microbes and virus are found on all worlds. Are other universes based on the same energy criteria? Our best hope of knowing is from Plasm.

Light stuff energy is photon electro-magnetic force (emf). But Dark energy and matter, *Dark stuff*, may be a geometric matrix, a substrate for Light stuff energy. Dark stuff *repulsion* seems to counter gravity *attraction* and may function independently of emf.

Gravity is considered space-time curvature geometry. And gravity *attraction* may then be considered *positive* curvature. Similarly, Dark-energy *repulsion* approximates *negative* curvature. Are gravity and Dark-energy spacial energy, geometry, or both?

*

Lela's first meeting is with a dozen kids preparing for puberty. They sit in a circle of the Lilith Longhouse atrium. Bamboo chimes ring softly. Water flows thru bamboo pipes. Lela asks the kids to close their eyes and listen to the sounds of wind and water.

A few minutes later, Lela asks the kids to open their eyes. She smiles as the kids yawn and rub their eyes. As she stretches so do the kids, copying her movements. She speaks softly:

"Over the years I often visit this tunnel-town, as I have close kin here. But of course, all people everywhere are kin (kids laugh). Please eye-blink-*on* your MindRecord to review our conversations afterwards. Y'all may call me or each-other on any point any time.

"We all go thru puberty. As we need to replace kids who move to off-earth tunnel-towns. Most kids move on as interns. I believe some of y'all will also. Some may choose to remain as interns here in the Atlanta islands. Everyone is needed, it's as simple as that.

"Puberty is an anxious and often painful challenge. As we become a new species, change is certain. As y'all are starting to realize, *change* is the one *constant* in life. If that sounds like a contradiction, it truly is. But so is life, and that's why we're here.

"Regardless of change, most people value and love life. It's not just a matter of replacing people. Ma's energy permeates the Cosmos and is expressed in nurturing all life, especially our kids. Does it make sense to say that puberty is part of energy recycling?

"Most of y'all are two years away from puberty and the seed-bank *Gathering*. The closer you get, the more complex the parenting tech gets. And the more complex it gets, the more interesting it gets. Parenting will transform y'all into skilled scientists.

"Back before the Cataclysm, accomplished scientists were known as doctors of philosophy, PhDs. Leave it to the patriarchs to demand social distinctions and status for all aspects of life. As with guy-religion, learning status fed the craving for wealth and power.

"With Ma's help we'll get y'all thru puberty. Let's meet here each week at this time. If a session is missed, check with one of us for an up-date. After each meet I'll go flying with anyone who wants to join me. Bring a flying suit or let me know if ya need one.

"Let's review some basic energy ideas: I'm sure y'all have heard Ma, Deep Mother-Cosmos is infinite and perpetual. Ma's energy is *Light stuff* electro-magnetics (emf). *Dark stuff* seems to be the emf scaffold. Ma endlessly recycles and transforms all cosmic energy.

"Energy beginnings and ends exist only in our imagination. Ma may be limitless, but at present our mental processes are limited. Our minds may be expanding to aid cosmic energy recycling, and to expand and benefit all life.

"*As energy is neither created nor destroyed, it must be endlessly recycled and transformed.* Cell energy recycling is the so-called *birth-death* cycle. Daily, billions of body cells recycle, are reborn, and coded. Longevity results from optimum cell recycling.

"We are part of Ma, Mother-Nature, Mother-Cosmos, and Great Mother Isis. Nurturing life enables Ma as she codes and recycles cosmic energy. Matriarchs do what comes naturally. And that is to support life, wherever it's found, and in whatever form.

"But y'all know this! Many folks imagine birth-death as shifting between dimensions, and maybe it is. Plasm electrons suggest lucid dreaming shifts dimensions. Recycling, recoding ourselves starts here at puberty, extending to nests throughout the Cosmos.

"Cosmic energy recycles our body. Billions of cells are replaced daily, yet our *sense-of-self* remains essentially intact, though constantly modified. Do dying cells code replacement cells? Plasm electron cell rebirth is part of cosmic energy recycling.

"Cell energy continually reforms mind and consciousness (C). About C, I imagine y'all browse WikiArchives (heads nod). Can anyone describe the Hard-Body Problem of C? Amazing that after a millenium, understanding C remains little more than theories."

Isis: "Gen, our last tutor, suggested some WikiArchive *look-ups*. *Consciousness* was one of the last she mentioned. Wiki suggests that the *Hard-Body Problem* is: *How does electron-neuron mind thinking energy arise from unthinking electron energy?"*
Lela: "How do complex thinking critters grow out of unthinking stuff? Do not assume electron energy is unthinking. All stuff may be sentient and conscious, to varying degrees, depending on energy complexity. Y'all think there's any non-thinking energy?

"Is consciousness a matter of degree, complexity, code, or linkage, as with wormhole web links? We say that all energy code is linked. And most believe that all energy is linked with a degree of consciousness. Are complexity and consciousness related?

"Before the Cataclysm, the question was often discussed: Are people *Real*, living in reality or are we *Sim*, simulations? Visitors suggest we are *Real* based on: the evolution of code complexity, adaptation to climate change, and surviving repeated cataclysms.

"Particle *entanglement* experiments suggest a persistent cosmic link. Change particle parity in one place and it's twin instantly changes, even if separated by millions of light years. To over simplify, a heads coin is always *entangled* with tails of that coin.

"About this time, someone asks: *what's a coin?* Can I assume y'all know about pre-Cataclysm money, coin? Money was an abstract crystalization, a bogus idolatry of patriarch power. Patriarchs were untrusting and traded in tokens of power, like money and guns.

"OK, so how do we perceive? How are we conscious of unthinking stuff? How does one's mind know the world outside itself? Consciousness understanding hasn't progressed much since the Cataclysm. There's many hard questions and few hard answers!

"Is there an objective physical world outside our perceived sensory awareness of mental experience? That's the inevitable question that arises. Or is the mind the sole creator of the physical world? Only sensory perception consciousness can create physical experience."

Hildi: "WikiArchives suggest sensory awareness perception result from neuron microtubule links that form consciousness. But *electron transfer* seems to be the basis of energy, existence, and consciousness. Is it the core of mind? Yet another hard question!"

Lil: "Consciousness seems to be a matter of degree. All beings and all stuff have some sensory equipment. All energy interacts, even Zero Point Vacuum and Microwave Cosmic Background radiation. The Cosmos is infinitely connected with or without our awareness.

"Even pre-Cataclysm heat sensing thermostats had basic sensory code for heat detection. All they could sense was heat, poor things (all laugh). Electrons *sense* a boost or loss of energy, from the gain or loss of a photon. Quarks and vibrating Strings may also sense."

Bern: "If Ma is living energy, consciousness may be complex entangled energy code. What provides a degree of consciousness for all forms of energy, if not some form of *electron transfer*? The code of life seems based on *electron transfer*.

"Mentioning Quarks suggests Vibration Energy Fields (VEF) as in String theory. Each perpetually changing VEF may create a new but short-lived energy particle or energy loop."

Lela: "*Electron transfer* energy code and VEF both make sense. But does the most complex energy code exist only in people? Genetic code can be compared from WikiArchives. We're still exploring an unknown Cosmos. What will the next world reveal?

"Genetic code provides vital proteins, 20 proteins are essential in people. Proteins and electrons are key to molecular interaction. Long before the Cataclysm, X-ray crystallography shed light in the area of genetic code. And electrons are the basis of gene activity.

"People have about 23,000 genes, and each gene has 30,000 DNA letters. Rice grass has 50,000 genes, each with 4,500 DNA letters. It's 53 million letters for people and over 54 million for rice. Both people and rice have similar amounts of genetic code, and so what?

"DNA letters code proteins via nitrogen nucleobase amines. Combo-duplicates of Cytosine (C), Guanine (G), Adenine (A), and/or Thymine (T) code proteins, form limitless organic life. Similar life code is found on all the worlds we've nested in so far.

"Does rice grass need the same sensory awareness as people?Probably not, but all plants can sense and chemically communicate danger. Plants sythesize code, depending on habitat conditions. So do plants have a degree of consciousness? Yeah! I believe so.

"The significance of code depends on molecular links in sensory cells. For the trillions of animal cells there's thousands of connections for each cell, and even more for brain neuron cells. The complexity of cell connections is only part of the mystery.

"Closer to home, we talk about patriarch sociopaths. We need not dig deeply to discover that testosterone was not the only factor contributing to patriarch aggression. While it was most important, pre-Cataclysm records point to many other contributing factors:

"Most significant are: 1) Climate change, 2) the Social-Emotional scaffold, 3) Vassopressin, 4) Cortisol, 5) Serotonin,6) Oxytocin, 7) Nitric oxide synthase, 8) Dopamine, and 9) Noradrenaline.

There's a biological basis for these, and probably other factors influencing patriarch behavior. Check the archives for the 2013 book by Patricia Churchland, *Touching a Nerve—The Self as Brain*, p. 145.

"For our next session, please research how these nine factors may interact with testosterone to influence aggressive behavior in both men and women. Hint: Oxytocin and Vassopressin affect mothers' ability to protect their young. *WikiArchives* is an excellent source!

"Consciousness seems to depend on hormone levels, as well as sensory neurons. In terms of sensory awareness and consciousness code, people were top predators before the Cataclysm. The role of top land predator now belongs to the house-cat size cheetahs."

Lil: "Planet Hestia life resembles phage virus and cyanobacteria. Hestia Cyano and phage form sentient clouds, much as they do on Earth. Life forms resembling Cyano and phage are reported on most worlds with human tunnel-towns. Is it cosmic geometry?

"All worlds studied utilize some form of DNA/RNA, but with complex variations. Many worlds have vast subsurface environments that are difficult to explore. The Cosmic Matriarch Diary provides reports of many such explorations on a daily basis."

Isis: "Reproduction is life recycling it's energy. At least I assume that's what explains genetic code. We're able to code electrons and other Light energy particles, but not the Dark energy scaffold. Yet all cosmic formations share the *mystery and beauty of being.*

"Rice grass adapted to land from water on Earth maybe 200 million years ago. Rice had more time to amass genetic code than did people. But rice accumulated far less DNA than people. Do species gather only the genetic code needed to adapt and survive?"

Bern: "Genetic code complexity provides both energy conservation and recycling. Sensory awareness, perception, and consciousness also seem to conserve energy. *Greening* is successful on many levels, but overall *Greening* succeeds since it conserves energy.

"Good point about the Dark stuff in all critters. Perhaps Dark stuff provides a scaffold for Light energy. Most important, Dark stuff may have a basic role in energy recycling and conservation. It may be that the Cosmos conserves energy so as to recycle it."

Lela: "I didn't intend to get so far afield. But yes, puberty coming-of-age is a human aspect of cosmic energy recycling. Seed-bank Gathering germ cells is cosmic energy recycling. *Our Place in the Cosmos* depends on how well we conserve and recycle our energy.

"It's also *Our Place in the Nature*. It's awareness of our part in energy recycling. In terms of code complexity, people and plasma electrons are the most complex and mysterious energy beings. We love mysteries. I believe the mind craves and needs mystery.

"As part of mystery, there's a craving for challenge, adventure, and risk. We seek unique experience. Noting recent comments in the Cosmic Matriarch Diary, what do y'all think about the question: Is patriarchy be an evolutionary disease?"

Jen: "Y chromosome male sex is hundreds of millions of years old. Certainly, male sex predates humanity in vertebrates, invertebrates, and even in microbes. It's known that sex hormones such as testosterone from sharks can even replace human testosterone.

"Life as we know it arises from electro-magnetism. Sex and all metabolic functions depend on positive and negative electrical charge. Energy transfer requires negative electrons and positive ions such as sodium (Na^+), as well as hydrogen protons (H^+).

"Hormonal errors are more likely at fault, rather than sex genes. Is it likely that Ma, Deep Mother Cosmos gave humanity toxic patriarchy 6,000 years before the Cataclysm? That matriarchs easily modify hormones says we're dealing with imbalance."

Lela: "Jen, that's a brilliant idea! But let's get back to basics. As we adapt to rapidly changing bodies, we must take more complete control of our reproduction. Ma has made pre-puberty training a necessity. So we must procede cautiously with incubator birth!
"Energy recycling is increasingly complex due to body and mind changes since Cataclysm. Before the Cataclysm, human reproduction was much like that of other mammals: Germ cells marinated in sex hormones, but less so now.

"Cataclysm survival and wormhole OrmNets encourage nesting in off-earth worlds. A thousand years of extreme *Longevity* and cosmic nesting transform *Homo sapiens* into *Gyna cosmos sapiens.* And what can we expect for the next 1,000 years? Dare we guess?

"A 1,000 years of adaptation forces gestation and birth out of our body and into incubators. In-body reproduction is no longer viable.

Our egg-sperm is optimized in seed-banks and as embryos. And skin stem cells are routinely adapted to culture embryos.

"We depend on incubator liners cultured from mother uterus cells. Puberty skills now include mastering birth techology. Puberty is far more than vision quests, ritual dances, and druming. Y'all need to learn seed-banking, tissue culture, and incubator tech.

"It's often said, but bears repeating: Our future depends on training to be parents and birth medics. We call it parenting and in our post-Cataclysm world, parenting is the most valued of all skills. In the last class a key challenge was fine tuning amniotic fetal fluid.

"Full-time parenting before the Cataclysm might have prevented the Cataclysm. Or at least more intensive parenting might have softened the hard edge of patriarchy. But *might-have-beens* are a waste. So why do I do it? Maybe its part of our human heritage.

"Comments about Dark energy code raise a good point. We code quantum and Light energy, such as photons, electrons, and neutrinos. Why not code the Dark stuff within and between all subatomic particles? Now there's a challenge for y'all.

"There's far more Dark than Light energy. Is Dark stuff truely the scaffold for electrons, protons, quarks, and neutrinos—the Light stuff? Light and Dark stuff are mixed even though there's far more of the Dark stuff. We ask the Visitors and they affirm that view.

"On Earth, countless neutrinos pass thru Dark energy, and pass unimpeded thru our bodies. Does Dark energy dominate all dimensions and universes? Here's another challenge. It's something else to think about and discuss, not that there isn't enough already.

"Before the Cataclysm, Dark energy was identified with Zero-point energy. Can it be coded in negative electron volts (-eVs)? As Dark energy expands, do we and all stuff expand? But we're making too many assumptions again. Another human flaw, if y'all collect them.

"Dark stuff seems to be geometrical. Could it be an analog of space-time, but without electrical charge? Dark-stuff may even be the scaffold-matrix for space-time Light-energy. Let's see what y'all come up with next week. Feel free to ask the Visitors!

"Getting back to puberty. Y'all have a great advantage over pre-Cataclysm kids. Pre-Cataclysm kids suffered from extremes of sex hormones. Moderation of sex hormones improves mind, body and longevity. Now with resident viral phage we monitor ourselves.

"Before the Cataclysm, puberty brought a flood of sex hormones. Many kids found themselves at a pathological edge that was never well understood. Sex hormones caused major social and global problems, especially out-of-control violence and suicides.

"Sex hormone extremes often became pathological, both for post-puberty teens and adults. Guys and gals frequently pursued each other destructively, due to hormonal cravings. Unless one lived thru it, it's impossible to understand it, and few understood it."

Hildi: "With phage virus auto-moderated hormones, we develop strong birth team friendships. Friendships are important for puberty and there's a sexual aspect to these friendship teams. Physically, our sex is various degrees of touching and feeling.

"Of course we have intimate friends. There is sexual attraction, but we don't lose control. We understand hormonal moderation is vital. We care equally about guys and gals. Nurturing and mutual caring is our primary concern. It includes oral and tactile sex play."

Lela: "Well done! Intimate teams are a vital part of birthing. Y'all have a couple of years before reaching puberty. With the onset of puberty y'all can contribute eggs-sperm to seed-banks. And quite true, sex play is an important part of pre-puberty and parenting.

"When adding eggs and sperm to seed-banks the designated birth teams are listed. Y'all can create birth teams at any time. In fact, all twelve of you can form a birth team core, but more is better. The number in a parent team is up to the gene parents."

Isis: "Archives before the Cataclysm note that virus epidemics, climate extremes, and overpopulation discouraged births. Population issues made my ma's team wait ten years before they were called for my birth. Is it always going to be that way?"

Lela: "Species density is a constant concern. The Cataclysm, a thousand years ago, was rooted in too many aggressive patriarchs. There were prior cataclysms. As far as we know, the 2026-2036 Cataclysm is the first man-made, and with the greatest lost of life.

"For eons people were guided by Mutterrecht, natural maternal law. It's Ma's, Mother-Nature's birthing law for all life. Naturally, the primary Mutterrecht issue is mother-child well-being. Since the Cataclysm, Mutterrecht is restored as the primary cosmic law.

"The Great Flood left few survivors. And they had to adapt in order to survive. Did increased testosterone promote the survival of aggressive males? It's far more complex than a single hormone. So let's not dismiss it as patriarch pathology. Truth is we're guessing!

"Archives suggest that 15,000 years ago rapid warming of the Earth resulted in the Great Flood cataclysm. Most likely some aggressive men survived. But earlier, mothers controlled births. Matriarch cultivation likely reflected moderate population growth.

"Over the millennia, matriarchs guided humanity, limiting population and technology to reflect available resources. It was thousands of years before the number of aggressive men could exert dominance. Again, the clues are few and uncertain.

"During Bronze Age patriarchy, tribes of militant Amazon horse-women resisted patriarchs. Over 1,500 years, Amazons resisted patriarchs. See what y'all can find in the archives concerning Amazon resistance. Look into *The Greek Myths* by Robert Graves.

"Aggressive men began degrading Mutterrecht and the Earth about 6,000 years before the 2026 to 2036 Cataclysm. As far as is known, the Bronze Age begins the era of patriarch tyranny. Amazon Goddess Hippa suggests horses used to resist patriarchs.

"Aggressive local leaders began the chain of global tyranny. Patriarch aggression and war-lord power-lust victimized all people. The Bronze Age begins with patriarchs victimizing each other. At the same time, victimization of women and children intensified.
"Patriarch power depended on people. As repeated in their scriptures: *Be fruitful and multiply.* It made women into breeding cows. The Great Flood likely traumatized survivors into a breeding frenzy. Children were seen as the path to wealth and power.

"Before the Great Flood, widespread matriarch leadership is suggested by the relatively large number of women and children remains found in ceremonial burials. Few men were found. Later Bronze age burials feature men and horses, with few women.

"Hormone levels before the Great Flood is unknown. Likely, some men with high testosterone reproduced. That may account for patriarch domination up to the 2026-2036 Cataclysm. A major part of patriarch tyranny was the *demonization* of women.

"The Cataclysm 1,000 years ago ushered in major changes. People and most land critter survival equate to nine females to one male. Ma recycles life energy, more to conserve quality of life than quantity. Often overlooked is the role of public health sanitation.

"Matriarchs learn from Ma. Elders born before the Cataclysm teach the need to limit population. Over-population wrecks public health long before destroying habitats. Pandemics hint at degraded public health. Anyone have examples of such problems?"

Hildi: "Satellite archives overflow with examples. Rodent and insect plagues were common all thru patriarchy. Well known are grasshoppers becoming locust when serotonin hormone triggers a plague of frenzied socializing. It's like patriarchs and testosterone.

"Patriarch greed mined the Earth for wealth, creating over-population. High birth rates were needed to build armies that must be fed and replaced. Matriarchs created the Mutterrecht family, but patriarchs perverted the family to serve their lust for power.

"Plagues began with lack of crop diversity. For matriarchs, birth limits, and food diversity depended more on horticulture than large scale mono-crop farming. Iroquois First Nation tribes are documented examples of earth-friendly diversity cultivation."

Lela: "Addressing over-population takes us back to the Cataclysm. It was less a problem of over-population, and more of hormonal imbalance. Hormonal imbalance produced sociopath leaders. The few women leaders were forced to mirror patriarch attitudes.
"The *beginning of the end* goes back about 6,000 years. Neolithic to Bronze Age empire building began canceling Mutterrecht. The transition is seen in myths of gods dominating goddesses and male dominated burial. Ancient societies are reflected in burial rites.

"Human species, as distinct from older primates, branch-off two to three million years ago. So-called *Modern* humans like ourselves, are about 250,000 to a million years old. Perhaps that's when plasm electrons began to make a neuron-mental difference.

"Mutterrecht (MR) amounts to natural cosmic law protecting parent-offspring. MR guides people and all life. That patriarchs trashed MR is a crime against both humanity and nature. A necessary correction was nothing less than the Cataclysm.

"Matriarchs provide MR for all life throughout the Cosmos. MR nurturing comes naturally, as it is coded in us. MR may be human-level cosmic energy recycling. Kids learn to nurture and support life. Malignant lust for power ended with patriarchs."

Hildi: "Nurturing is biological energy recycling. Mother-child must always come first, for all life. We see this with animals and plants. Our place in the Cosmos is understood in terms of MR. It makes all gals and guys cosmic midwives."

Isis: "In the patriarch Bible there's a story of brothers Cain and Abel. Abel grows the livestock. Cain grows the crops. Their god favorably receives Abel's burnt flesh offering, but not Cain's crop offering. This leads to Cain murdering Abel, as the story goes.

"It's a fable of conflict over resources: water, land, and people. The Bible details the constant warfare between patriarch tribes. The patriarch gods preferred burnt flesh offerings. Pre-Cataclysm records refer to burnt meat offerings as Bar-B-Qs." (All laugh)

Lela: "Excellent y'all! I could not have come up with a better summary. Keep in mind that Ma, Mother-Nature has the last word. Think of Ma's Great Flood and the Cataclysm as gifts of nature. Yeah, patriarchs loved Bar-B-Qs, often craving burnt flesh.

"Ma provides survivors who remember. We move forward with code that takes us to other galaxies, to the heart of Mother Cosmos. We realize now why Ma provides nine gals to one guy. It seems related to *insular dwarfism*, reduced land supports fewer critters.
"Over the next week, please think about what y'all can do in preparing for the great energy transition to puberty. We'll talk about your puberty preparations next week, same time and place. Now grab flying suits. Let's fly over the tunnel-town forests."

They make a fast exit. Graphene wings flapping in the tunnel breeze, the kids fly behind Lela, as she follows the tunnel gulls. Everyone is laughing and shouting. Tunnel-towns on new worlds try to vary the breed of flora and fauna from Earth.

The hundreds of worlds with tunnel-towns are selected to the extent they provide earth-like growing conditions. New worlds meet Nanobot search code criteria for oxygen, water, mountains, and electro-magnetism. All such worlds have earth-like life forms.

No matter how earth-like a world may be, human habitats are confined to tunnel-towns in caves and lava tubes. Fusion tunneling begins where OrmNet wormhole Portals intersect a world. Portals are usually in or near natural cave or lava tube entrances.

Tunnel-towns are created both to protect native life, as well as human life. The utmost care is taken in providing ventalation and water filtering for tunnel-towns. These precautions are taken before earth-life is introduced in the tunnels.

When tunnel habitats Secure Human Life (SHL) then plants and animals are tested on a limited and controlled basis. With SHL complete, then flora and fauna habitats are extended as the tunnels expand. Tunnels extend in ten-mile circuits of one mile segments.

Along with other tech skills, tunnel technology (TT) is vital for human survival. Pre-puberty kids learn the importance of TT skills, as well as parenting technology (PT), and the other technologies that contribute to our place in the Mutterrecht Cosmos.

MUTTERRECHT

It's hard for pre-puberty kids to grasp the fine points of cosmic energy recycling. Yet kids learn that *birth-death* is part of cosmic energy recycling. But they could care less at that age. It's up to parent teams, stewards, and tutors to help prepare them.

Elders go easy on kids. Few could grasp Mutterrecht (MR) until after the Cataclysm. *Our place in the Cosmos* requires awareness of our role in cosmic energy recycling. With plasm electron Visitors, human awareness and consciousness grows rapidly.

One thousand years after the Cataclysm, Visitors help shape our MR consciousness. Plasm electrons expand and deepen our mental faculties. At the same time, Cyano and other microbes transform people into a new species: *Gyna cosmos sapiens*.

Biological explanation alone cannot account for our expanding consciousness. Matriarchs believe that it's Ma, Deep Mother-Cosmos transforming *Homo sapiens* to *Gyna cosmos sapiens.* The process of becoming a new species began with Ma's Cataclysm.

On Earth, cataclysms occur every 15,000 years, or so. These are due to climate, tectonics, volcanos, asteroids and solar phase shifts. Earth cools, ice melts, and waters flow. The Great Flood warming cycle15,000 years ago passed as many lives as the Cataclysm.

Over millions of years of adaptation, each cataclysm recycled energy, and renewed life. MR is the cosmic law of life. MR is human-level life energy recycling. Plasma electrons, Cyano, and other microbes expand the complexity of life.

Over a 1,000 years, it's known that many cosmic visitors, meteors and asteroids among them, seed life thru the Cosmos. In addition, plasm electrons and microbes, other seeds of life are perpetually dispersed. Ma also provides more complex beings, such as people.

MR is living conscious cosmic energy based on cosmic energy code. Ma's energy code has neither start nor end. It is energy code that endlessly transforms and recycles. Most likely, MR and all life energy disperses as cosmic *Panspermia*.

Cataclysm survivors evolve as *Gyna cosmos sapiens*. Adaptive evolutionary changes result from radical climate shifts. Most likely, Great Flood survivors 15,000 ago experienced radical changes. Surviving males were likely more aggressive than before.

Patriarch aggression was at least partly due to hormonal imbalance. Matriarch Mutterrecht was gradually suppressed by the increasing patriarch victimization of women. Patriarch violence played-out over the 6,000 years prior to the 2026-2036 Cataclysm.

*

Explaining to kids is a challenge. Understanding cosmic energy recycling is complex enough. Elders living long before the Cataclysm are the primary stewards and tutors. Understanding our place in nature is a stretch for everyone. Some will never get it!

We're challenged both mentally and physically. Surviving since the Cataclysm over 1,000 years is our extreme reality. Yet we know that *our reality is only the perception of this instant.* Some Elders call extreme longevity *the long march of instant reality*.

Too often solitude is treated with suspicion. At times, Elders crave solitude with nature. Some people may feel the need to take solo wormhole jaunts, for a change. Matriarch caring can be over-done. Excessive *in-your-face* nurturing can be anxiety provoking.

Since longhouse living began soon after the Cataclysm, solitude is not highly valued. With so few survivors it was vital to extend family *nurture* to all. In this regard, Elders surviving the Cataclysm are assigned as *Grans* for kids born after the Cataclysm.

Half the people on Earth are *Elders*, born before the Cataclysm. The other five-million born after the Cat are considered *Kids*. Most kids prefer starting life as interns in off-earth tunnel-towns. And replacements for those going *off-earth* are always needed.

Most kids want to explore the secrets of the Cosmos, Mother-Nature. Before the Cataclysm this was termed child's play curiosity. Matriarchs now view it as a budding scientific attitude. But kids must provide egg-sperm before interning *off-earth*.

Parents, stewards, and tutors encourage kids' exploratory curiosity. It starts with *Childhood*, the time between weaning and the start of pre-puberty training. Older kids learn to *nurture, care,* and *guide* younger kids. But all kids may freely chose post-puberty paths.
Pre-puberty tutoring starts with nine to ten year-olds, depending on readiness. Longhouse teams of about twelve are trained: to donate egg-sperm, in incubator-birth, as parent teams, for life-span skills, cosmic exploration, as well as tunnel-town building and nesting.

*

Increasing longevity began long before the Cataclysm. Before the Great Flood, 15,000 years ago, a Matriarch Golden Age is described. A Matriarch Age is said to have lasted a million years. It's thought to be an early appearance of multiple human species.

The patriarch era vastly reduced life-spans. Hormonal aggression led to over-population and increased mortality. Women and children were the primary victims. Over-population began with patriarch gods and the biblical command: *Be fruitful and multiply*.

Soon after the Cataclysm hormone modification was promoted for longevity. Some hormones help Elders care enough to stick around and contribute for 1,000 years, or more. If Earth is not enough, there are OrmNet portals to a virtually unlimited array of worlds.

Excess testosterone led to the patriarch sociopath disaster and Cataclysm. Moderate levels of testosterone are needed for growth of brain, nerves, muscle and bone. Over ten-times moderate levels caused faulty judgment, poor reasoning, and extreme aggression.

Patriarch warlord sociopaths caused 6,000 years of Bronze Age war and suffering. Women and children were the primary victims.

Testosterone clouded the judgment and thinking of global leaders, causing: over-population, pollution, and finally the Cataclysm.

*

Ma, Mother-Nature restored ten-million of the prior billions. And of those who survive and thrive, there are nine gals for each guy, for people and most other land critters. It's Ma's adaptation to a radically changed Earth, providing a Mutterrecht renewal.

Now that Earth is a tropical water-world, hormonal moderation naturally prevails. But matriarch stewards insure that body biochemistry remains moderated. Over-population, pollution, and patriarch excess are relegated to the dust-heap of antiquity.

It's natural that kids, especially pre-puberty kids, seek adventure in new worlds. Preparing kids for new world nests is what Elders do best. A vital part of that process is parenting preparation. Kids learn birth skills as they prepare for OrmNet nests in new worlds.

*

Life energy has *death-birth* as a junction in cosmic energy recycling. Matriarchs sense that all energy is alive. But until they reach puberty, kids seldom care about birthing. Kids are mostly into friendships, games, skills, technology, and adventures.

Parent teams, stewards, and tutors have their work cut out for them, transforming kids into birth teams. Games transform into birth teamwork. Kid learn to play with birthing skills. Kids are guided by Elders, but mostly they learn to train each other.

Cosmic energy recycling supports people and all life. It amounts to Mutterrecht (MR) flowing from Ma, Mother-Cosmos Mother-Nature. Our numbers are limited on Earth and on nested worlds. And that too is part of MR cosmic energy recycling.

*

By 2036 the Cataclysm left Earth a tropical 99% water world of ten-million. Earth was cleansed of pollution and patriarchs. Also washed away are rockets, nuclear fission, hoarding, property, and greed for power. To share, care, and nurture life is now our goal.

MR is nurture, caring, and kindness. These values were globalized after the Cataclysm. The first century opened the OrmNet wormhole cosmic web to exploration and nesting. Motivation was and remains to plan for the next Earth, and new world cataclysm.

Undersea fusion boring extends living space on Earth. But fear of the next cataclysm extends coded NanoBot drone search for viable worlds. Ten centuries later, millions of people nest in hundreds of worlds, mostly in the Milky Way and Andromeda galaxies.

Stewards limit Earth to ten-million people. It's the number surviving the Cataclysm. New world tunnel-towns are limited to 10,000 people. NanoBots probe for viable worlds. So as to protect surface life and human life, all off-earth nests are tunnel-towns.

*

We realize that the human body is rapidly evolving. *Adapting* may be a more accurate term. Everyone jokes about our stick-insect mantis-like body. Joking is healthy and encouraged. A humor-laden culture grows throughout the Cosmos, mostly via HoloVids.

Early-on, kids learn how human bodies change. They're surprised at how much *lower-body* organs dominated people before the Cataclysm: *They looked like fat slugs before the Cat* is a typical comment. We ask that kids be kind to our ancestral memory.

For ten centuries lower body organs continue to shrink. Body hair is virtually gone. Lower body mortality-morbidity is just archives. Lungs, blood, nerves and the brain quickly adapt. Aided by plasm electrons, our minds can now range far into the Cosmos.

Hair folicle micro-insects evolve into symbiotes and benefactors, as do the trillions of body microbes. It's hard to distinuish between the *original* and *enhanced* portions of people. But our mental enhancements are mainly from plasm electrons, the Visitors.

Cyano, Cyanobacteria skin photosynth began for people going from the Earth into the Cosmos. As we become *Gyna cosmos sapiens,* skin photosynth energy systems are increasingly fed by radiating solar-luna drones in tunnel-towns, on and off Earth.

Cyano skin implants began as a chloroplast tattoo fashion after the Cataclysm. In the first century, most Elders experimented with stem-cell skin photosynth. At the same time, graphene flying-suits were becoming popular. People were joining avians in flight.

Flying-suits give us bird-like freedom. But flying requires far more energy and oxygen than surface or even under water activities. Skin photosynth provides additional oxygen and energy. Gastro-intestinal energy is largely replaced by skin-solar radiation.

Cyano clearly extends human longevity. Before the Cataclysm, few people lived beyond a century. Direct mind to gene access is enhanced by Cyano and plasm electrons. Ma makes Cyano into a cosmic aid, in transforming life energy and species.

Virus phage along with Cyano provide photosynth adaptation. As we become a new species, we lose body mass but gain in height. Minds expand outside the body. We're becoming telepaths, sending mind packets thru the wormhole OrmNet to off-earth Portals.

Our human seed remains fertile, but embryo, fetus, and infant must now mature in uterine tissue-lined incubators. Parent teams get at least two years of birth training. Multiple skin stem-cell embryo duplicates essentially eliminate birth mortality and morbidity.
In-body birth is no longer viable. But there's been no incubator mortality-morbidity in centuries. But parent-team anxiety remains for birthing at all stages of technology, from embryo to infant. Birth teams consist of dozens, up to an entire long-house of 100.

In the first training month, pre-puberty kids are immersed in cosmic energy theory. Fractal Energy Granules, cosmic scaffolds, and recycling geometry are studied. Plasm electron interaction with *consciousness* imaging is now a vital form of mind projection.

Distinctions are carefully made between sensory awareness, perception, and consciousness. Prior to the Cataclysm, brain-nerve electron transfer was considered *subjective*, while cell electron transfer was viewed as *objective*. Now there's no distinction.

Electron *fields* inside and outside body and mind are studied. And electron *waves* are now documented. Electron energy is transferred via Adenosine Di Phosphate (ADP) and Adenosine Tri Phosphate (ATP), in nerve tissue synapses and in all living cells.

Pre-puberty *deep cognition* involves mastery of cellular electron energy dynamics. Birth teams become practicing geneticists and biochemists. They become adepts at incubator skills. They learn to parent their kids. Kids learn to parent their parents and each other.

Parent teams, by working together, come to realize that the energy of mind, life, and Cosmos is shared. Kids soon learn that all energy is alive. Depending on code complexity, all forms of energy may be conscious, from quarks and electrons, to people and worlds.

We continually examine the relation between human complexity, cognition, and consciousness. Consciousness expands as humanity adapts and evolves into *Gyna cosmos sapiens*. Increasing cognition and mind travel seem to result from increasing code complexity.

It's known that plasm electrons and Cyanobacteria, along with virus, have a key role in adapting life on Earth. Ma, Deep Mother constantly transforms this energy. Ma shapes the Cosmos, recycling and reforming electron energy on her cosmic wheel.

Electron waves of about 40-hertz stimulate neuron oscillations and consciousness. An early clue was the use of anaesthesia to temporarily block peptide micro-tubule nerve signals. At timed intervals, the micro-tubules unblock and consciousness returns.
Micro-tubules open or close the Neuron Voltage Gate Protein Ion Channels (Channels). Active or inactive Channels alter the electron potential of sodium, potassium, calcium, and chloride ions. Altered neurons selectively block or unblock pain and consciousness.

What's known of consciousness is that electrons, Channels, and nerve micro-tubules are involved. These provide electron: sensory perception, awareness, experience, imagination, consciousness and a sense-of-self.

Electron transfer energy functions in cell ion Channels, trillions of times per second in people and most all critters. Electrons are the key energy source for life as we know it, on Earth and in all tunnel worlds. Kids must learn this before puberty.

Before the Cataclysm, physicist Roger Pensrose had a similar theory: Quantum collapse of brain neuron electron waves is traced to brain *protein micro-tubules.* It may be the basis of conscious experience. Plasm electrons seem to be part of consciousness.

*

Longhouse stewards constantly impress kids with the importance of limiting births. Hands-on birth skills require about two years working in birth teams. Kids learn that everything is energy, including people. Ma, Deep Mother is the ultimate cosmic source.

Kids learn to transform Ma's energy into new people. The major hurdle is understanding and transforming their own egg-sperm energy into new life. Birth teams effectively recreate themselves. As they recreate people they become Ma's acolytes.

Initially, longhouse kids form birth team *friendships*. Teams may consist of 50 or more from the same or neighboring longhouse. As *in-body* birth has not been viable for almost 1,000 years, human survival depends entirely on *out-of-body* incubator technology.

Over 1,000 years since the Cataclysm, Ma equips people for nesting in the Cosmos. We're becoming a new species: *Gyna cosmos sapiens*, recreating ourselves as life stewards. Kids call us cosmic park rangers. Anything for a laugh, or just a smile, is fine.

I meet with the kids once a week for a few hours. As they approach puberty, their team work and parent birth skills grow. Two years are needed to see themselves as parents. When they are able to donate viable egg-sperm to the seed-bank, they are ready.

Since the Cataclysm kids mature earlier. Many kids talk within a few months of birth. Reading, thought projection, and reception within six months of birth is reported in the Cosmic Matriarch Diary. Infants and cheetah kits nurture each other when paired.

Infants of three months have been placed in nursing pens with mother cheetahs and kits for an hour daily, over a month. Parent team observers note 20% faster maturation for infants and kits, compared to infants and kits that were not paired.

It seems that human adaptation and evolution are accelerating. It's hard to say if it is rapid adaptation or evolution. But evolution certainly depends on adaptation. Research stewards believe that plasm electrons, Cyanobacteria, and virus phage are all involved.

Physical body change seems eclipsed by mental development. It may be that these changes are triggered by both the Cataclysm and the resulting *Insula Dwarfism.* Kids are trekking the wormhole OrmNet at earlier ages. Now small groups are going *walkabout.*

Younger kids are involved in NanoBot drone coding. Many send out programmed NanoBot drones seeking intern posts in wormhole linked galaxies. Kids are *playful* at earlier ages, seeking adventures in new worlds, and especailly with cheetah kits.

Pre-Cataclysm archives suggest that earlier maturation began late in the 20th Century. At that time increasingly younger kids were becoming computer coding adepts. Maturation now speeds-up, is more widespread, and at an earlier age since the Cataclysm.

*

The latest kid rage is culturing *Slimes* that is plasmods (*Physarum polycephalum*). Slimes create fractal mazes, geometric networks leading to earth-like worlds. Slimes are Protista that lack brains or nerve cells. Yet for billions of years Slimes survive unchanged.

Slimes recycle the energy of decaying plants and microbes, especially decaying trees. Slimes solve intricate fractal mazes leading to decay and sustenance. It's similar to coding NanoBots to find viable earthlike worlds. It suggests a cosmic geometric unity.

Slimes suggest the geometric unity of cosmic energy. Fractal math and geometry are shared by plants, animals, fungi, and protists like Slimes. Slimes seem to exhibit the shared geometric code of all cosmic energy, from micro virus to mega galaxies.

THE COSMIC GAME

Preparing pre-puberty kids as parents works best as a team sport. Birth training is parent-team work. Wormhole OrmNet Portals to new worlds make birthing skills a cosmic sport for kids. As new seed donors, kids are welcomed to off-earth worlds as interns.

Kids are trained as parents and interns, both on- and off-earth. Each year kids apply as interns to tunnel-town worlds in Milky Way and Andromeda galaxies. Half the kids in parent-teams prefer to intern on Earth. But local seed-bank deposit takes priority.

Many kids prefer being interns in tunnel-towns that plan nests in new worlds. Kids plan Visits, Vision quests, and Walkabouts to wormhole worlds. But first visas or invites are needed. Worlds that want more people eagerly extend visas to recently fertile kids.

Interns are accepted only after they donate seed on their home world. And most worlds only accept interns pledging seed to host worlds after local donations are complete. Naturally, off-earth tunnel-towns prioritize their own seed-banks for contributions.

*

Why kids are so curious about life before the Cataclysm is hard to figure. Birth tutors, born before the Cataclysm, are constantly surprised by kid curiosity. Abundant archives are kept from before the Cataclysm. Kid-play often includes *surfing* thru the archives.

The usual comment, when kids are asked about pre-Cat archives is: *So many people, like fat grubs ... so much wasted land.* It's hard enough for nine-year-olds to understand one Elder living a millennium, let alone half of Earth's ten-million as *Super Grans.*

Kids ask: 'What was it like for you personally?' I tell them the truth. I was part of the two-thirds of people that enjoyed a charmed life in a privileged part of the world. My first century as a guy was more of a psychological challenge, rather than physical.

The gals in my life created me in mind, body and spirit. Mother, grandmothers, aunts, teachers, and cousins, all guided me to a *good life*. And I contributed to their lives. But two mates of over 58 years were most special. Both passed relatively young from cancer.

Living a century as a guy, the gals in my life fired my imagination and desire to be a gal. It was a slow process, taking a full century. But it was my deep life-long desire. I vividly recall my gal-related experiences of nurture, love, and long-term affection.

Certainly, there were some guys early in my life. My dad, uncle Bob, and a few friends provided nurturing much like the gals in my life. Is it that guys' envy of gals is part of the patriarch problem? Now, teams of gals and guys share parenting.

Pre-Cataclysm gals mostly suffered with live birth. Gals were only in partial body control. Much of birth suffering resulted from the patriarch envy of women. Yet most guys deeply admired gals. Now both gals and guys are dedicated parents and matriarchs.

In contrast with post-Cataclysm longevity, the short lives of the 6,000 year patriarch era was likely a mind-body health problem. During that era, the few guys indoctrinated in the anti-gal envy cult became patriarch leaders. The majority of people were gals.

The ten-million Cataclysm survivors developed intense long term imagination, creating a universe energized with the love of life. Folks know this universe as the Mutterrecht Cosmos. If y'all have survival theories, please share in the Cosmic Matriarch Diary.

Consciousness seems to create the Cosmos. Most Elders had some childhood ills, typically: colds, flu, measles, mumps, chicken pox, and whopping cough. Even with these, I lived as a guy in relative good health. But my skin and sinus were highly sensitive to fungi.

My first century ills consisted of: GAD, General Anxiety Disorder, intermittent sinusitis, and hyper-sensitive skin. These were manageable as I shaved my head and face hair daily. Now, we've replaced body hair with our beautiful bronze cutin-carapace.

Surviving the Cataclysm has been a radical change for Elders and kids alike. The best part of survival for me is becoming a gal and freedom from hormonal imbalance. No longer suffering excess sex hormones is a great relief. Not GAD, but some anxiety remains.

At each weekly parent training session for the kids, I begin with a story from my experience before the Cataclysm. Trying to explain billions of people surviving on land continents covering 30% of the Earth, is a challenge to say the least. But kids love the stories.
The Cataclysm ended by 2036. Earth is now 99% Mother-Sea. Ma, Mother-Cosmos gave Mother-Earth a much needed *facial*. Earth is now tropical with a dozen small metro island chains. Ma ended over-population, pollution, and patriarchs. We keep it that way!

Ten-million people now thrive on Earth. More than half are Super Grans from before the Cataclysm. People and most all land critters now live with nine gals to one guy. It's considered the result of severe climatic change, initiated by the Cataclysm.

Before the Cataclysm, it was called *Insular Dwarfism*, the result of major land mass reduction. *Warming* climate eventually reduces body mass and the number of survivors. But *cooling* favors increased body mass, as was with Ice Age mammoths.

Longevity is the result of: nine-gal to one-guy ratio, plasm electron Visitors, Cyanobacteria tattoo photosynthesis, and *Insular Dwarfism.* But we are most grateful to Ma's Cataclysm tsunamis that washed away population, pollution, and patriarchs.

Nine gals to one guy is still hard to understand. But a majority of gals for all critters was a trend long before the Cataclysm. In spite of patriarch toxicity, gals always seemed to be central to the focus of Mother-Nature, and at the core of all kinship relations.

Love of gals began as far back as I can recall. Love of ma, sister, aunts and mates defines my first 100 years. My heart's desire was achieved when I finally became a gal, due to the Cataclysm. Gals are favored by Mother-Nature for obvious survival reasons.

Transition to a gal gets me thinking of the ancient Pinocchio story. The wooden puppet had one all consuming wish. It was to become a real boy. And for me, it was to become a real gal. Living the *good life* provided both Pinocchio and me with our heart's desire.

*

Over the millennium, Earth's people were limited to the original ten-million survivors. Only those leaving Earth are replaced. With few passing, new births replace kids moving off-earth. A 10,000 person limit is suggested for each of the many off-earth worlds.

Off-earth nesting strategy anticipates cataclysms. Along with longevity, tunnel-town longhouse living, and limiting population, also contribute to cataclysm planning. We're far better prepared, knowing cataclysms can be expected any time, on any world.
Ma's cosmic game perpetually recycles and transforms cosmic energy. Cataclysms and life transformation are part of cosmic recycling. So too is nesting in tunnel-towns throughout the Cosmos. Kids' seed-banking is a vital part of energy recycling.

Kids learn birthing, parenting, and nesting. Within the framework of the *Great Cosmic Game*, kids need to absorb the technology. Aided by plasm electrons, minds are increasingly able to directly access genetic data, expanding our mental abilities.

Direct gene access provides a broader and deeper use of cosmic code and energy. The need to more deeply grasp cosmic energy relations is a vital part of pre-puberty training. Plasm electrons are another of Ma's great gifts. It's taken long enough to realize this.

Kids begin pre-puberty training with an Energy Intensive. They're prepared with the reality of cosmic energy as they learn parenting. Belief in Ma, Deep Mother Cosmos starts with the idea that:

Cosmic energy is neither created nor destroyed. But energy is endlessly transformed and recycled. We become Gyna cosmos sapiens so as to nurture cosmic life. Accepting Mutterrecht means that we are a nurturing part of life energy, and the Glory of Being.

Kids were asked to look for pre-Cataclysm mention of an *endless* cosmos. Sending code-bots and web-crawlers found an interesting clue written by Sean O'Casey in a 1949 autobiography published as *Innishfallen, Fare Thee Well,* page 15:

The Endless Endlessness of Eternity .... Where all the aging ages shall be but as the time wasted in the blink of an eye; and the life of the longest lived universe shall be to them less than the life of a bubble afloat in the swift air.

*

Ma, Mother-Cosmos, Mother-Nature doesn't care what we say or think. Ma just *keeps-on keeping-on.* She just keeps playing her great cosmic recycling game. We are all Ma's avatars, acolytes, stewards, and enablers of life-energy in the worlds we nest.

Elders train kids in puberty prep circles. On newly nested worlds, trainers are often invited from Earth to train local stewards. Elders willing to teach from experience about pre-Cataclysm life are most welcomed and valued.

Elder stories from before the Cataclysm are greatly valued. Many of these are dramatic HoloVids. Elders attempt to *make it real.* Challenges, successes, and failures are part of the many stories in the Cosmic Matriarch Diary, all part of the Great Cosmic Game.

Elders, Super Grans like Lela volunteer to train off-earth pre-puberty kids. It's an opportunity to tour new worlds. Elder trainers can give kids a first-hand sense of life before the Cataclysm. Elders training includes detailing intern and parenting options.

Training kids to be parents provides an intimate learning experience with incubator birth skills. It relates parenting to cosmic energy recycling. Parent teams start as strong child friendships. The point is for teams to contribute their seed to the seed-banks.

Kids learn about pre-Cataclysm birth and the changes imposed by the Cataclysm. Pre-Cataclysm patriarchs showed little regard for people or the Earth. Patriarch birth planning amounted to: *be fruitful and multiply*. Birth planning is now energy recycling.

Life on Earth, and in the Cosmos, is ultimately the domain of mothers. Ma's energy is perpetually recycling. Ma exists in the *infinite present*. As such, Ma is past, present and future. The Cataclysm transforms Earth mothers into cosmic matriarchs.

Ma adapts *Homo sapiens* to become *Gyna cosmos sapiens*. Cosmic walkabout is feasible via OrmNet wormholes. Becoming cosmic stewards means nesting throughout the Cosmos. Matriarchs speculate that plasm electrons provide cosmic consciousness.

*

Anthropologist J. J. Bachofen called Mutterrecht (MR) the first religion, the *Ur-religion*. As elaborated in his 1861 treatise *Das Mutterrecht*, *Mother Right: an investigation of the religious and juridical character of matriarchy in the Ancient World*.

Matriarch transformative energy provides nurturing for people and all life. Mothers' nurturing is the scaffold for MR. Mother-Nature's energy recycling is parental nurture raised to a cosmic level. These are core values presented as a part of pre-puberty training.

Parental feelings grow out of team nurturing, thru pre-puberty training. The transformation is from *subjective* energy into the *objective* energy of parent nurturing. It is made objective in seed-banks, births, and tunnel-town nests throughout the Cosmos.
Kids learn the relation between energy, nurturing, and life. Options and probabilities are continually discussed. *The only certainty is change*. As tunnel-town nests expand in the Cosmos, the reality of a thriving matriarch-based cosmic humanity increases.

Pre-puberty kids learn that *probability* is more realistic than *certainty*. Real-time probability exercises deal with incubator-birth skills. Kids learn that energy reality and probability are inseparable. But cosmic probability has no room for certainty.

We also play the cosmic game by adopting ecosystems (ecos). Parent teams and Elders adopt ecos. Lela has adopted an eco centered on felines and cheetahs. Some kids assist her in daily recording feline observations. Cyanobacteria (Cyano) is one eco.

Other adopted ecos are rodents, beetles, owls, kudzu, and bromeliade flowering plants. All families of life are adopted for intense study, as well as protection. Cyano are studied as the source of our Being, and source of chloroplast skin Greening.

Lela's first session with the kids of the Isis longhouse deals with cosmic energy. She prepares kids for their role in the great cosmic game. Kids become *players* in the game of stewarding cosmic life. It's all part of cosmic energy recycling.

Lela: "Please *blink-on* your MindRecord for each of our sessions. Let's meet here each week at this time for about three hours, including breaks. Bring flying suits and we'll get air-born after each session. Anyone adopt an avian eco, any bird folks here?

"By now y'all are becoming players in the great cosmic game of energy recycling. Y'all now have an idea of what we're doing. My goal is to provide hands-on training in the skills of incubator birthing, parenting, as well as interning on new worlds.

"Understanding the nature of energy, reality, and consciousness is as good a starting point as any. I'll provide guidance, but *we all get by with a little help from our friends*. Mutterrecht tells us we're part of one energy family, and learn best from each other.

"Here we are, thirteen friends preparing to birth new people. We're creating paths to new worlds. We know Ma, Mother-Cosmos will send a cataclysm to recycle the energy and transform the world we've come to know and love. It encourages and energizes us.

"We expect Ma's little surprises while preparing for really big ones. Before the Cataclysm, we said that *a mother's place is everywhere.* Mothers recycle the flow of energy and of Beings.

"Now we say our place is in the entire Cosmos. OK, tell us about our place in nature, in terms of energy, anyone?"

Gina stands and Lela nods in her direction to speak.

Gina: "It's likely that the Cosmos, Ma, is infinite endless energy. So all of us, all stuff, our thoughts, imagination, consciousness, and reality are all forms of energy. Since being an incubator fetus, sleep-tutors primed our minds with the basic stuff we need."

Lil: "Even before the Cataclysm, it was known that *energy is neither created nor destroyed, but is endlessly transformed*, in other words: *recycled.* Based on the nature of energy conservation, Ma is timeless with neither beginning nor end."

May: "*Time* is an invention of our imagination. If we assume Mother-Cosmos, Ma, is timeless and infinitely recycling energy, then Ma's energy will transform endlessly. The variety of energy forms are also infinite. Are people just another energy form?

"Our last guide suggested we do a *look-up* of the role of *Being* in pre-Cataclysm art. Ancient authors dealt with Being in two main ways: first, in the life or death sense, as in Hamlet's *To be or not to be.* But later philosophers treated Being as existence.

"Sartre's *Being and Nothingness* deals with Being in the existential sense, that is '*to exist.*' Heidegger uses *Dasein* which in old German means '*being there in the world.*' Mutterecht views the Cosmos and all energy as Being, without possibility of non-being."

Jan: "It makes sense that cosmic energy is personified as Ma, the great *ever-creating* mother. Archives state that our first mothers had similar views. First mothers worshiped Mother-Earth, a Fertility Goddess, a Great Birth Mother, and a Sky Mother.

"Matriarch imagination suggests people are Beings, in the sense of creations of perpetually transforming energy. Like clay potters, people shape mental electron energy into consciousness and reality. Imagination creates a vast array of mental experience."

Bern: “The first million years of humanity must have been a matriarch era. Ma the Great Goddess, Cosmic-Mother, Mother-Cosmos is the ultimate focus of human attention and gratitude. Ma lives in our energy, hearts, and minds, as well as in our genes.

“After the Great Flood cataclysm, 15,000 years ago, patriarch tyranny tried to replace cosmic Ma with a cosmic Pa. But Ma is in our trillions of cells. Ma is our Being. Women were victims since the Bronze Age, until the Cataclysm solved our issues of Being.”

Lela: “Y’all are off to a great start. Between sleep-tutors, kin, archives, Cosmic Matriarch Diary, and direct mind-to-gene access, much of our training is well along. Also, check-out WikiArchives, if ya haven't yet. Any thoughts about pre-puberty training?”

Isis: “Maybe you’ve already planned for it, but most of us hope to intern as part of parent teams that are already functioning in neighboring longhouses. We have kin that are already in parent teams. We might learn as interns by helping active parent teams.”

Lela: “Good thinking, y’all. Intern talk was to start at the second session. But y’all are far enough along to begin now. OK, so between today and our session next week, same time and place, try to find active parent teams that need more people.

“The most desirable parent teams are those who donated seed to a seed-bank and devised parent team schedules. They will need more people to fill their schedule. Contact local seed-bank stewards. They can steer y’all in the right direction.”

*

Bern: “In researching the antiquity of matriarchy, I found a beautiful and enlightening book from a few decades before the Cataclysm. It provides a vision of the earliest known matriarch civilization on Earth. It’s title is:

Continuity and Transformation of the Goddess in the Indo-European and Christian Eras, THE LANGUAGE OF THE GODDESS, by Maria Gimbutus, 1986, especially page 318:

The clash of Old European with alien Indo-European religious forms is visible in the dethronement of Old European goddesses, the disappearance of temples, cult paraphernalia, and sacred signs, and drastic reduction of religious images in the visual arts.

This impoverishment started in east-central Europe and gradually affected all of central Europe. Aegean islands, Crete, central and western Mediterranean regions continued Old European traditions for several millennia more, but the core of the civilization was lost.

This transformation, however, was not a replacement of one culture by another but a gradual hybridization of two different symbolic systems. Because the androcentric ideology of the Indo-European was that of the new [patriarch] ruling class, it has come down to us as the "official" belief system of ancient Europe.

Old European sacred images and symbols were never totally uprooted; these most persistent features in human history were too deeply implanted in the psyche. They could have disappeared only with the total extermination of the female population.

Goddess religion went under-ground. Some old traditions, particularly those connected with birth, death, and earth fertility rituals, continue to this day without much change in some regions; in others, they were assimilated into Indo-European ideology.

Lela: "In my own time, before the Cataclysm, *Mother-Mary, Mother of God, and Mother of Mercy* were just a few of the terms that patriarch priests could not eliminate. It would have been like eliminating ones' mother. Anyone want to comment on this?"

Bern: "*Androcentric* patriarch ideology became the "official" belief system not only in Europe but in most of the world. Under the illusion of 'God the father' patriarch religion and widespread murderous persecution of women took place throughout Europe.

"Patriarch tyranny, in prior centuries resulted in female genocide. Millions of women were tortured and exterminated during the

Burning times of the *Witch* persecutions. The persecution of women became a wealth-generating industry for patriarch leaders.

“Strangely, patriarch religions published the details of these genocides. They took pride in their tortures, or so it seems. And they left abundant records detailing their crimes against humanity and nature, documenting a new low for patriarch inhumanity.

“It was a widespread mental derangement, a virulent social pathology. What would we call it today? It was deeper than genocide. It was a cancer of the human spirit, the poisoning of human consciousness. It’s for all to view in WikiArchives.”

Kim: “Yet the Goddess persists, not only on Earth but throughout the Cosmos. During the worst of patriarch persecution, public adoration continued for: Mother Mary, Mother of God, the Holy Mother, Mother-Nature, and many other Goddess incarnations.

“And up to the time of the Cataclysm, global health care was dominated, tyrannized actually, by patriarchs. Patient survival from women surgeons, was far greater than from men surgeons. Medical statistics detail these differences in gender health care.

“Many deaths per 100,000 births were considered normal, in all nations, before the Cataclysm. Compare that with ‘not a single birth death in over 1,000 years.’ Matriarchs have much to be proud, but improving the quality of all life, I believe, is our high-point.”

Lela: “Now with parent birthing teams, seed-banks, and embryo to infant incubator nurturing, suffering, mortality, and morbidity are relegated to the patriarch dust-heap. And Good riddance! As parents, y’all serve Ma, the Goddess, and Deep Mother-Cosmos.

“We pride ourselves on nurturing and caring for all symbiotic life. But most pride is directed to maternal care. Before the Cataclysm patriarch greed discouraged people from having kids. Patriarchs made it so difficult to raise kids that global populations declined.

“While matriarchs were concerned with the *quality* of the family, patriarchs were most concerned with family *quantity*. How much wealth could the family generate? That was the over-riding issue for patriarchs.

“The patriarch *demon* is in the details. Searching pre-Cataclysm news, on October 25, 2022 a report that ‘*deadly maternal conditions* were among the top five killers of women under the age of 20.’ And many *structural murder of women* reports exist.”

BACK IN THE DAY

It's more than a 1,000 years since the Cataclysm. On Earth, ten-million now thrive, of the billions that passed-on. Matriarch *nests* thrive in many worlds and galaxies. But Milky Way and Andromeda galaxies still house most of the tunnel-towns.

Kids like to joke that matriarchs are now the *cosmic park rangers*. But the *wise-cracks* are quite perceptive. We truly are cosmic park rangers, nurturing symbiotic life where ever we find it. Matriarch stewards promote life on Earth and in all of the off-earth worlds.

Naturally, tunnel-town nests are limited to earth-life compatible worlds. Nesters don't disturb surface life, but do explore surface life remotely. Earth life is limited to nests in tunnels, caves, and lava tubes. People support planet surface life by non-interference.

What life forms have NanoBots led us to? Off-earth worlds now host millions of people, and share similar life forms. All life forms are electron-based and much like Earth microbes. Off-earth life can be complex, often defying people's penchant for classification.

As on Earth, electrons and microbes form complex life. All the trillions of cells in people, and all life on Earth, are based on microbes and electrons. Plasm electrons power all life found so far. This is the case on all worlds explored to date.

Since *off-earth* tunnel-towns began as preparation for the next cataclysm, matriarch survival planning has been quite successful. It's taken millennia to realize that similar Beings create all life. Is it accidental that similar Beings are found on all worlds?

Archives show periodic cataclysms have renewed Earth at about 15,000 year intervals. In peopled tunnel-town worlds, geological cataclysm evidence is common. Nesters suspect that more complex and savvy life forms are wisely hiding, as is the case in the Earth.

Long before the 2026-2036 Cataclysm, it was widely recognized that *Energy is neither created nor destroyed, but is endlessly renewed, transformed, and recycled.* Most Elders think of cataclysms as renewals, but few kids think this way.

Life that is renewed by each cataclysm inherits genetic code better suited to its adaptation. Genetic code adapts and evolves mainly to encode nerve systems and brains. As Beings evolve genetic code, learning by adapting to their habitats, consciousness also evolves.

Both mind and genetic code seem to adapt and evolve, while expanding consciousness. Consciousness energy code also adapts, expands, and recycles. The consciousness energy of all life is part of Ma, Deep Mother-Cosmos, perpetually recycling.

Consciousness energy may be outside the constraints of plasm electrons. As life and consciousness adapt, some forms may learn to bypass the constraints of electron mass. Consciousness seems photon-like, outside the constraints of mass, body, brain, and mind.

A millennium since the Cataclysm, plasm electrons continue to adapt to the neurons and cells of people. That may explain our rapid cosmic evolution to becoming a new species: *Gyna cosmos sapiens.* We are becoming both organic and electron Beings.

Pre-Cataclysm archives claim many human species preceded *Homo sapiens* over a period of millions of years. Adapting and evolving to changing habitats is necessary for any surviving species. And *Gyna cosmos sapiens* is likely not our last change.

Biologists say that no new brain cells are added after birth. Yet all of the trillions of body cells are recycled many times during the life span of people. Recycled body and brain cells must adapt to the ever-changing body and brain habitats, becoming new cells.

The *infinite present* includes both the past and future. With neither beginning nor end, what appears as *birth-death* is an energy transfer point. Cosmic energy perpetually recycles from one form to another. But is there life energy beyond the electro-magnetic?

Consciousness enlivens the Being of all energy. Distinctions seem to arise from varying degrees of energy code complexity. Reality for all Beings may depend largely on consciousness code. Yet consciousness like energy seems dispersed throughout the Cosmos.

Cosmic renewal events are aspects of cosmic energy recycling. Just as billions of our body cells recycle and are renewed daily, so too are life forms constantly recycled throughout the Cosmos. It's all part of Ma renewing and recycling her cosmic energy.

Elders alive since before the Cataclysm thank Ma, Deep Mother-Nature, Mother-Cosmos. Ma's cosmic recycling creates (Micros) micro-beings. These include Cyanobacteria (Cyano), Phage-Virus (Phage), and Plasm-electrons (Plasms).

Micro and Plasm energy transform into living cosmic energy, the basis of life. Micros are found in all worlds in which people nest. Complex Earth life is based on the energy scaffolding provided by Cyano, Phage, and Plasms. Mind-resident Visitors confirm this.

NanoBots are coded to search for: 1st, traversable wormholes, 2nd, orange to red dwarf stars, 3rd, rocky water worlds, 4th, Carbon, Hydrogen, Oxygen, and Nitrogen (CHON) worlds, and 5th, if no Micros are found, Cyano and Micros are automatically seeded.

*

These are the lessons about energy that pre-puberty kids must learn. Are Cataclysms and supernovas thoughts in the mind of Ma, Deep Mother-Cosmos? And do people comprise the mind of Ma? Perhaps all thoughts are Ma's, as we're part of Ma's Cosmos.

Cataclysms recycle life-energy on Earth. Novas and supernovas recycle star-stuff into galaxies and the various star systems. The elements of life are forged in the crucibles of stars. All cataclysms and supernovas may be viewed as cosmic recycling activities.

And since the last of these, the Great Flood about 15,000 years ago, patriarchs provided a steady flow of violence, suffering, plagues, wars, and genocides. Matriarchs believe that patriarchs on Earth violated Mutterrecht and cosmic energy recycling.

Does Ma care? Is Ma conscious of what happens on the Earth, or in any part of the Cosmos? It's not likely. But people care and may be the mind of Ma. Is Ma's sole purpose to churn, transform, and recycle energy into new energy and new life? It seems so!

The patriarch war against nature is long over. And the Earth will eventually be transformed into yet another form of energy. But Ma provides matriarchs with the creative consciousness energy to nurture life and nest in worlds throughout the Cosmos.

*

Elders need to record their pre-Cataclysm memories. In this year 1036 AC (After Cataclysm, 3036 in the ancient patriarch calendar), we need to record the human experience. WikiArchives, Cosmic Matriarch Diary, and CosmNet HoloVids fall short.

Stewards suggest systematic synthesis from earliest mems. Mems may be recorded, stored, and transferred by means of personal MindRecord. But Stream-of-Consciousness (SoC) mems occur naturally, providing a freshness often lacking with other mems.

For memory retrieval, plasm electrons are suggested. These can be directed to gather experiences long before the fourth-year of life. Electrons energize mem neuron micro-tubules. Egg donor parent mems are transferred to infants, especially math and music.

Lela provides her initial entry as an example, using SoC:

Lela: "My earliest mems are from age two or three. But using plasm electrons, mems prior to birth may be retrieved. Brain tissue before three-years is not well defined. Infant mems are hazy, seldom worth the effort. But parents often provide infant mems.

"My ma repeatedly told people how she suffered with my birth. She was in labor over the last twelve hours of May 31, 1936. With great pain and difficulty, I was born early on June first, a large eight-pound guy. And in my first hundred years I lived as a guy.

"Maybe it was the painful birth experience that soured relations between ma and me. We loved each other. But our anxious nature made it hard for us to tolerate each other for extended periods. But widely spaced short visits worked well.

"My relations with dad were far better. He better understood our anxiety. After dad passed, I never said as much, but I felt that ma could have done more to extend dad's life. Ma could have stopped smoking around dad. But smoking wasn't well understood then.

"By my 100th year, my body chemistry, if not anatomy, transformed to that of a gal. Mother-Nature and my strong desire finally helped me become a gal. But that's a tale for another time. Many guys had similar desires, but few satisfied them.

"As for infancy mems, only two minor events emerge. At about one-year, dad caught me by the pants as I crawled out a first-floor open window. At two-years I jammed the large "J" handle of a men's umbrella in my mouth. Dad told me these tales.

"Ma often repeated her memory of my birth: *At birth he was the ugliest thing I'd ever seen. With clumsy forceps, he was bruised black and blue. Did that butcher of a doctor birth a changeling, I asked. He was not expected to live. But look at the beauty now!*

"Between ma and dad's parents there were nine aunts, five uncles, and many cousins. All were loving. But I was closest to ma's sisters. They were like a team of parents. Before my sister Roxy was born, I spent lots of time with gram, ma's mother, and sisters.

"Gram's house on Marion Street in Brooklyn had three levels. Aunt Fran, Uncle Si, and cousins Evy, Irv, and Jack lived on the top floor. Aunt Min, Uncle Ot and cousins Bea and Pearl lived on the middle floor. Often I stayed with Gram on the main floor.

"At age four I recall asking Gram why everyone had such short names. Laughing, she told me that they were poor and could not afford longer names. I recall laughing with her at the time, sensing it was a joke. Aunt Laura said, 'the Irish love telling tall tales.'

"Sister Roxy (Ro) arrived when I was five. Ro's was an easier birth than mine. Ma asked me to watch my sister when she was busy. Minding Ro was a joy, as I recall. Soon after her birth a full color nursery rhyme linoleum floor was placed in the room we shared.

"It had illustrated nursery rhymes: Jack Sprat, Miss Muffet, Old Woman in the Shoe, Jack and Jill, Humpty Dumpty, Cat and Fiddle, Mary Mary, Mary's Lamb, My Son John, Old King Cole, and Jack Be Nimble. The rhymes provided early reading lessons.

"Over many hours I sang and danced the rhymes for Ro. In time with my singing, Ro laughed and jumped around the crib. After a year of this, ma could stand no more and she ended the entertainment. I think it was on or about the start of school for me.

“Ma and her sisters often described themselves as nervous. I thought ma was especially nervous. It was called *high-strung* back in the day. Ma’s kin all did wage work. They did not have an easy life. But they did not suffer any deprivation that I’m aware.

“As an adult, the family nervousness I shared was called *anxiety*. Before the Cataclysm, I believe *anxiety* became a global mental health issue, especially among the wealthier nations. Constant wars and economic stress were the main causative anxiety factors.

“Anxiety was perhaps the least toxic product of patriarchy. As with most patriarch ills, anxiety was a *profit center*, and an important part of the patriarch global health industry. With General Anxiety Disorder (GAD), patriarchs profited up until the Cataclysm.

“GAD severity varied. For me and many others GAD was relatively mild. Physical symptoms were sinusitis and cortisol flow rhinitis. But GAD contributed to a life of sharpened awareness, perception, consciousness, memory, and attention to detail.

“Thinking back, dad’s anxiety likely resulted from his angina heart condition. He cared deeply for his family and kin. In spite of, or because of, his illness dad was always kind and nurturing. Mutual kindness, caring, and nurturing by all my kin was my life lesson.

“My aunts were consistently *present, loving, and nurturing* to all kin, as well as to their own family. I recall the uncles as being *less present* much of the time, in contrast to my aunts.

“Dad encouraged my life-long habits of *Body Building* and pursuit of learning. My life as a guy and as a gal has been long and charmed. I continue seeking mental assets rather than material.

“Early on, I trained my attention to detail as a GAD benefit. A millennium later, GAD is now termed Hyper Perceptive Awareness Syndrome (HPAS). Rather than a mental *fault*, HPAS is considered a mental *feature*. Matriarch nurture makes all the difference.

“Now we realize that matriarch civilization, culture, and social nurturing have eliminated most causes of worry, fear, and anxiety.

Optimal health longevity, exploring the Cosmos, and securing tunnel-towns in many worlds, relieves most of our anxiety.

"A 1,000 years after the Cataclysm, we're becoming a new species, *Gyna cosmos sapiens.* In terms of adaptation and evolution, this pace is quite rapid. Cyanobacteria, Phage virus, and Plasm Electrons are credited in transforming people into a new species."

*

Lela: "My dad had a heart injury over the last 20 years of his life. For his health dad moved us to South Florida. He died at age 52, when I was 18, starting at Emory university. My medical interests arose from dad's bad heart and continued in pre-med thru college.

"I was born a battered but fairly typical guy, and remained so until I reached my centennial in 2036. It was the year the Cataclysm ended. My life in Atlanta began as a gal Energy instructor. And for the first time in my life I felt a sense of comfort as a woman.

"Early-on, I prepared myself for the health sciences. After graduating Emory, my interests included Philosophy, Networking, and Political Economy. In New York City, I was hired by New York University for diabetes research at the NYU Medical School.

"Shortly after, I met my first wife on a rush-hour train, going to work. Standing near her seat, Bev smiled at me and that was all it took. We had 41 happy years and two sons. She died of cancer in January 2000. But the Cataclysm ended the global cancer plague.

"Bev was an enterprising genius. With her artistic skills and interest in tribal art, she created a tribal arts trading company in Afghanistan. It lasted five years until ended by the Russian invasion in 1980. Bev helped many Afghans to escape the war.

"Admitted to first year Miami Medical School, I had twice failed basic college Physics. That ended my medical school pursuit. But I remained as a medical health researcher and instructor. A key perk working at NYU was unlimited free graduate level courses.

"Whenever I think of failing Physics, I think of two incidents with ma: I'm four-years old, playing with a neighbor boy. The boy had wonderful toys, but he urinated on his toys. When his ma became aware, he pointed to me as the culprit.

"In spite of life-long denial, my ma never believed me. I kept insisting that the boy pissed on his own toys. She believed she lost the boy's ma as a friend because of me. About the same age, ma took away my favorite blue truck, saying it's 'for a poor child.'

"It was all part of ma's life-long negative attitude toward me. As far as she was concerned, I was her life-long affliction. Nothing I ever did changed her attitude. Ma gave her affection and attention to her gal kin. For ma, guys were her source of life-long pain.

"Looking back, I think ma's negative attitude was directed more to men in general, rather than me specifically. The men in ma's life made her suffer: her father and two husbands died, kinsmen like me and her brothers were not available when needed.

"On the other hand, I think of the positive loving nurturing ways ma treated me. She drilled me in reading, writing, math, spelling, and speech: for 'th' and 's' sounds. Ma loaned me and Bev money to buy our starter house. I'm forever grateful to ma for that.

"This story details family complexity before the Cataclysm. Matriarch families are now simpler and kinder. Patriarch addiction to wealth and greed created most, if not all family ills. Comparing pre- and post-Cat family is like night and day, or war and peace.

"Three years work at New York uni (NYU) Medical College, earned a Masters in Philosophy. But my interest was in Political Economy. I also took graduate Biochemistry and Physiology courses. I spent over 20 years in health related research work.

"My first corporate work was in food and animal research. Broiler chicken was a major part of the food industry. Billions of broiler chickens were grown yearly as food in 6-8 weeks. It was research designed to speed healthy chickens to market.

"Dr. B, head of the Agricultural Division and I were of German farm family background. But I could translate Dr. B's German research papers from Swiss corporate research, while he could not. We had a friendly productive working relationship for years.

“As he said when he hired me, insisting on calling me Pal, ‘Pal, your language skills are like the cherry on the sundae.’ Meaning he greatly valued my skills. It was the start of a mutually beneficial partnership lasting during my entire corporate tenure.

“Dr. B and I did favors for each other, over and above our work. Major favors gained me promotions. Most of the favors involved getting animal body parts from slaughter houses. Most difficult was retrieving cows’ rumens, their four-part stomachs,.

“My corporate years included work as a market developer. I helped develop: potentiated sulfonamides to replace antibiotics, food and animal nutritionals, as well as sodium bicarbonate (Bicarb) buffers for environment and waste water reclaimation.

“Adding 7% Bicarb to the diet of ruminants increased milk fat and meat production by 10%. Bicarb aids roughage digestion, metabolizes bovine rumen methane bacteria. Rumen methane is converted into acetate, increasing dairy and beef protein.

“A Swiss corporation paid for my Masters degree in Marketing Economics, and a Doctorate in Political Economy. My thesis analyzed the Global Economics of the Family: specifically with the *Benefits of the Mutterrecht Family.*

“I worked toward an Economics doctorate at the New School for Social Research, begun by philosopher John Dewey. And I studied with students from all over the world. Most students were preparing for roles in their nations’ anticipated revolution.

“Patriarch leaders usually had the world in a turmoil. Exploited people attempted to rid themselves of autocrats. But patriarch autocrats led most all nations. My interest in economics focused on the basic role of the Mutterecht *family* in global dynamics.

“Patriarchs didn’t see Mutterrecht as valid. They opposed putting mothers, women, and children first. Pie-in-the-sky notions of a Cooperative Commonwealth were often promoted. But patriarch greed and power always came first, with human needs last.

“Before the Cataclysm, millions hoped for an Earth that shared resources in common. But patriarch power lust would never allow it.

Given this reality, the Cataclysm was needed to renew a golden age of Mutterrecht and bring about a Cosmic Commonwealth.

“I absorbed the love, nurturing, and faith in family from my women kin. Growing up with a communal sense of family created my goal to: *Extend the better nature of the Mutterrecht family into the Cosmos*. Family serves to nurture and recycles cosmic energy.

“As we’ve come to realize with family, Mutterrecht (MR) is the *angel of our better nature*. MR reaches more deeply than just nurturing mothers and children. MR not only reaches the core of the human family, but now nurtures life throughout the Cosmos.

“The longhouse is a Mutterrecht family, serving our communal needs. *We give to the family as needed. And receive from the family as they are able to provide.* Now, all people are nurtured and cared for within the many family longhouses throughout the Cosmos.

“Archives suggest a Matriarch era of at least one million years, prior to the Bronze Age, 6,000 years before the Cataclysm. But people survived patriarch and natural cataclysms. Matriarchs protect earth-life with wormhole OrmNet nests in many worlds.

“Cataclysms occurred during the first million years of humanity, and the billions of years prior. Ma, Mother-Nature recycles, adapts, and transforms life to fit the constantly changing habitats. And to preserve life we now adapt to tunnel-town living.

“It may be that Cosmic Family Geometry (CFG) secures tunnel-town life. And cosmic consciousness may be the source of CFG. All this may vary with energy code complexity. Electron energy may be part of, or even the ultimate source of cosmic geometry.

“Ma creates many cosmic family types, such as forms of: geometry, energy particles, elements, and microbes. The code of life transforms in complexity as energy recycles. And *Family* shapes the scaffold, the living energy geometry of the Cosmos.

“These rather obscure Energy discussions are admittedly highly: theoretical, philosophical, and even mystical. But objective energy trials are limited. Researchers must reach a point where self-questioning provides little more than instinctive insights, guidlines.

*

Energy speculation brings to mind my first research job with a diabetes research team. The current quandary over cosmic energy is reminiscent of the far-reaching issues with diabetes in the late 1950s. Diabetes was an issue until ended by the 2026 Cataclysm.

I'd recently graduated from Emory in Atlanta, giving up my place in the first year Miami Medical School class. I had free access to New York uni graduate courses, as a key perk in the NYU Medical diabetes research team. It was my *back-door* entry into science.

Slowly, I learned that diabetes was much more than a health problem. There were deep political, social, and economic issues. One-third of Veterans Administration funds went toward diabetes.

Our diabetic research was funded by drug companies. Clinical trials showed sulfonylurea (SFU) as an effective diabetes drug. SFU aided prediabetics and mild diabetes cases, not severe type 1.

SFU was first tried as an antibiotic. Folks with bacterial infections often blacked-out or went into coma, which suggested diabetes. SFU proved more helpful in relieving diabetic symptoms than as an antibiotic. Understanding diabetes was my first challenge.

Elaine P. Ralli, MD was our diabetes research group leader. As a medical doctor she studied and taught Nutrition Diabetes. Nutrition was not a required subject, but diabetes was fast becoming a leading global ailment. Her emphasis was mainly on diabetes diets.

In the 1950s, neither nutrition, diabetes, nor women doctors were highly regarded. In her 60s at the time, Doctor R. was my first encounter with a Medical Matriarch. She was a mental giant, a tough-minded clinical scientist, in spite of her small body.

At first I was slow to grasp the research value of our work. But I mastered diabetes clinical skills, married, took courses in Organic Chemistry, Quantitative Analysis, and Philosophy. Foolishly, I fantasized that medical school was still a possibility.

Replacing a guy who left for graduate school, I learned to take blood samples from diabetic out-patients. It was a 40-hour work week, with Monday and Wednesday mornings taking blood from diabetics at the adjacent Bellevue teaching hospital.

Doctor R. admired my skill and nurturing care with patients. Ability at getting blood from often failing and recessed diabetic veins was my main skill. In spite of an under active thyroid and a few lab screw-ups, Doctor R. was my constant supporter.

Decades later I realized that my under-active thyroid was most likely Generalized Anxiety Disorder (GAD). In the 1950s, there was little or no recognition of GAD, or even of anxiety. But the thyroxine tabs Doctor R. treated me with was probably helpful.

Many of the matriarchs encountered now, a thousand years later, exhibit the sterling qualities I recall with Doctor Ralli. The qualities of matriarchs were always present, but they were forced to keep a low profile until the Cataclysm liberated all of us.

FAMILY as SOCIAL STATE

As a trainer of pre-puberty kids, it's vital that I prepare them as a birth team family. Typically, kids enter our little group at nine years. They'll spend two years training to become a birth team family (BTF). Functional BTFs may have dozens of team-mates.

It's vital that kids learn how Ma, Deep Mother-Cosmos energy functions. Ma perpetually recycles cosmic energy. Cosmic energy has neither beginning nor end, but is endlessly transformed. And people are just one of the infinite cosmic energy transformations.

Ma is both cosmic mind and cosmic energy. It's not surprising that many life forms are also thinking beings, perhaps even people. That there are many conscious thinking Beings in the Cosmos, suggests Mother-Cosmos as the creator of Cosmic Consciousness.

Ma's mind consists of countless energy beings, with thoughts that are orders of magnitude greater than those of people. The cosmic mind may consist of numberless thinking beings. Electrons seem to be the vitalizing force of all life in the Cosmos.

We learn Ma's energy code as we form families. Families consist of: code, energy, elements, animals, plants, minerals—on and on. People initially formed families within tribes, clans, and as survivors adapting to habitats. *Ma is the ultimate source of family.*

For people and all critters, first families were of gals and guys. Mutterrecht folks now include all people. Patriarchs imagined: tribes as social states and nation states. But matriarchs revive the original *Family* as a primordial Soc*ial State* of cosmic geometry.

*

Birth teams form when kids can donate viable egg-sperm, or stem cell (Seed) to seed-banks. Birth teams are put on a longhouse birth readiness list. It may be years before a longhouse needs more people. All longhouses have seed-banks and infant incubators.

Longhouses lose kids most years. Once kids donate to a local seed-bank, they often choose to intern on other worlds. Interning is most popular, but kids may also Explore, go on Vision Quests, or Walkabouts. Wormhole OrmNet provides many off-earth options.

A millennia passed since the Cataclysm. The Family Social State now expands into the Cosmos. We are one of many families of living energy. As Ma, Mother-Cosmos recycles energy, complex forms arise. Families of life vary depending on code complexity.

Most familiar are biological families. These include microbes and photon plasm electrons that create people and all life forms. Life is: animals, including people, plants, microbes, fungi, protista, plasma electrons, genetic code, and consciousness.

The electro-magnetic plasm family includes: photons, electrons, ions, and plasma. Plasma energy is the most common type of cosmic matter. Plasma and microbes form the *scaffolds of life*. Depending on code complexity, all life is conscious, to a degree.

For all life, Mutterrecht (MR) is the *family* social state. MR is Ma's, Deep Mother's cosmic priority for safe-guarding mother and offspring. For life as we know it, mothers are the core of home and family. In other universes and dimensions it may be far different.

The mother-family is the source of fertility. Mother-family as *social state* is the basic scaffold for living cosmic energy. Nations and city states were patriarch tyrannies of over-population. But the family as social state is a cosmic creation of Deep Mother.

*

Knowledge of family and energy is a basic part of pre-puberty training. Kids need to understand why they go thru these rigors. Human survival depends on acceptance and performance by well-trained parent birth teams.

On Earth and in other worlds, all longhouses perform a vital training function. As the human body no longer supports live birth, intensive training in out-of-body incubator wombs is needed. We strive to improve the *quality* of people, but not the *quantity*.

In this year 1,000 AC (After Cataclysm), Earth's Cataclysm motivates people to nest in the Cosmos. The Cataclysm ended in 2036, after ten years of washing away all but *one-in-a-thousand*. Mother-Nature gave Mother-Earth yet another *make-over, face-lift.*

Earth is now a glorious tropical 99% water world. Out of the prior billions, ten-million people thrive on a dozen chains of small metro Earth islands. With many millions thriving in tunnel-towns on hundreds of worlds opened by the cosmic wormhole OrmNet.

Land life is much reduced, for people and other critters. But life in Mother Sea thrives. Since the Cataclysm, *nine-out-of-ten* critters are female. A warming Earth and reduced land seems the cause. It's all speculation as more research will always be needed,.

Gals were 90% of survivors, suggesting that Mutterrecht (MR) guides life. Nurturing symbiotic life is the only MR guideline. MR suggests a ten-million limit on Earth, and a 10,000 limit in each new tunnel-town. Limitless births yielded a toxic patriarch world.

Environment is a major concern. The Cataclysm cleansed Earth of population, pollution, and patriarchs. Many millions now nest in tunnel-town worlds in the Cosmos. OrmNet Portals throughout the cosmic wormhole network keeps us in touch and relatively secure.

*

Earth's diaspora began with the realization that cataclysms on Earth occur at about 15,000 year intervals. Earth archives document few cataclysms. Reports from nested worlds indicate similar cataclysmic events may be expected on all worlds.

In the first decade after the Cataclysm, surviving metros began fusion-tunneling under Mother Sea. Cataclysm shock and tunnel fusion tech made tunneling a priority. A millennium later, under-sea tunneling extends the Earth land habitat to almost 10%.

The *quantity* of land life is reduced, but *quality* increases. With plasms and microbes, human minds expand on Earth and into the Cosmos. Select land critters also benefit, as sea life proliferates. Islands and tunnels have become plant and animal extravaganzas.

Tunnel-towns are usually one-mile segments with safety partitions. Segments duplicate both sun and moon with programmed drones. Typically, segments have ten longhouses with extensive plant and animal habitats. Small forests and gardens are popular vocations.

Plasm electrons and microbes are considered to be the basis of life. Microbial spores and cysts travel the Cosmos, usually as part of space rock *visitors*. Beings similar to plasm electrons, virus, and Cyanobacteria microbes are found on all longhouse worlds.

On Earth, all life including people seems based on microbes. Trillions of body cells are built on the energy scaffold provided by microbes and electrons. *Both literally and figuratively, our bones link stars to stones.*

These and related data are suggested to kids being trained as parent teams. Much of what they learn is researched by the kids themselves, from abundant library and satellite databases. As the centuries pass, younger kids seem to be learning faster.

*

As Lela continues the energy training, she suggests a short pit-stop break. She asks for questions as the kids return from the break.

Lil: “Your kin were totally different from ours. I realize you’re talking about times before the Cataclysm, over 1,000 years ago. Kids now share in longhouses and large parent teams. But it does seem similar to your experience growing-up with many kin.

“Your ma was really different compared to our embryo mothers. Of course, stem cell embryos were coming into use before the Cataclysm. But birth of in-body fetuses was still wide-spread. My question is, do you see similarities between your ma and ours?”

Lela: “Well that’s really got me thinking. In some ways, my ma would have loved our MR world. My ma never said, but I know she thought that *women must endure, and men must be tolerated*. My ma would have loved the help provided by a parent-team.

“For most of her day my ma was on her own. Ma was stuck with the bulk of child care, shopping, cooking, cleaning, after school tutoring, and the countless daily *stop-and-start* household tasks. Wage work dad was gone from morning to night six days a week.

“Like my folks, everyone had to endure the worst of patriarch society. Few people understood hormone imbalance before the

Cataclysm. Dad did his best in view of societal abuse. Comparing now and then is like comparing day and night."

Isis: "Back in the day, were you aware that your mom and other women were suffering from patriarch abuse?"

Lela: "Another good question! I'd say 'yes and no.' In spite of our differences, I loved and respected mom. But like most women, mom was a patriarch victim. Example: patriarch culture said it was unfashionable to breast-feed infants, to keep one's youthful figure.

"Neither me nor my sister were breast-fed. Mostly poor rural mothers breast-fed. Patriarch culture pushed commercial infant formula in place of natural colostrum. Formula hindered immunity, increasing morbidity and mortality, such as childhood illnesses.

"Women were victimized constantly. Patriarch abuse was largely by means of commercial exploitation. War and the global greed economy were the most toxic aspects. Earth and all people were victimized. But women and children suffered the most.

"Cleaning-up the patriarch toxins required nothing less than a Cataclysm. Ma, Mother-Nature did what millions with the best intention could not. Ma cleansed the Earth of population, pollution, and patriarchs. Of the now thriving ten-million, 90% are gals.

"My sense was that ma and my women kin did the best they could, given the circumstances. Like settling for infant formula, smoking was propagandized as the fashion. While that abuse greatly increased suffering, it also increased patriarch wealth and power.

"Let's get back to talking about energy. But if y'all have any questions that can't wait, please feel free to ask-away. We'll treat your questions like breaks. Can't have too many breaks!"

Lela continues the pre-puberty energy discussion:

"Cataclysms are *direct* results of asteroids, meteors, and other sky visitors, heavenly stuff (laughter). Also, solar and polar magnetic shifts cause major climate changes. Cataclysms may spare those able to adapt to new habitats. Do families contribute to survival?

"*Indirectly*, families can reduce the deadly nature of habitat cataclysms. Here again, family *nurture and care* can save people. Simply seeking higher ground or a secure tunnel can make all the difference. Family is a social state more intimately than nations."

Jena: "Lela, your granma's family home almost sounds like a model for our longhouses. Does that make sense?"

Lela: "Yeah! Regardless of how stressful the day, family can provide a refuge. That's what I experienced with my kin, with my ma, as a guy with wives, and especially with our longhouses. Dad's passing, still left us with many kin in our family social state.

"A longhouse family and birth team provide family refuge. These provide us with a humane social state. When anxious or confused, family and kin can provide comfort, and a cushion or buffer.

"Iroquois and other tribes developed longhouses long before us. Long standing tribal clans are essentially large successful families. Longhouses are intimate and tangible family social states. Notice that longhouses are both independent yet cooperating, like clans.

"The Atlanta metro islands support under a million people, and longhouses support about 100. Earth's longhouse families are kinship clans and family *social states*. If y'all are stressed, your longhouse or birth team may be your most comforting *home*."

*

The Cataclysm put most people, land, and land life under Mother-Sea. But on balance, Earth's most pressing problems of over-population, pollution, and malignant patriarchs were resolved. Does the wormhole OrmNet bounty of new worlds compensate?

Many matriarchs attribute *thought* and even *intention* to Ma, Deep Mother-Cosmos and Mother-Nature. Many metro island chain stewards view Ma as our *guardian angel.* That seems reminiscent of pre-Cataclysm patriarch religious propaganda.

Cosmic consciousness (CC) like the Cosmos, is infinite. CC transforms life energy, as perpetual recycling. *One-in-a-thousand* people and land critter survival, along with 90% gal survivors, may seem intentional. More likely natural adaptation recreates people.

Many examples of warming habitats favor the birth of gals. Some snake and lizard species are only gals. Female parthenogenesis was most frequent in amphibians, reptiles, and sea critters before the Cataclysm. Now it's seen in land mammals since the Cataclysm.

The Cataclysm left mothers in charge, by default. We've returned to what may be the natural condition of life. It's again an age when mothers create family from the chaos. It's a new Golden Age and Mutterrecht has become the vital core of cosmic consciousness.

Cosmic guardian angels are most likely the microbes and plasm electrons that are at the core of life. It's known that Visitor plasm expands and links minds to genetic code. Microbes guide us thru wormhole portals into new worlds. Surviving is now thriving.

Even the transition from inactive microbial spores, in the near vacuum of space, and into active microbes requires transforming energy. Transformation requires the adaptation energy provided by the electro-magnetic energy of water.

But this is not news. Prior to the Cataclysm, it was known that Cyanobacteria (Cyano), Phage Virus (Phage), and lightning Plasma Electrons (Plasm) bring complex life to Earth. And similar life are seeded thru the Cosmos. This is reported on all nested worlds.

Cyano is often called Ma's *Cyano-Apple-Seed*, after the ancient *Johnny-Apple-Seed.* Microbes are found, in many forms, in all nested worlds. NanoBot drones continue to detect new worlds for new tunnel-town nests. All nest worlds support earth-like beings.

Microbes may be at the complexity limit of life found so far. Many are grateful that Ma limits life complexity on the worlds we've nested. How nurturing would we be to find life as complex as ourselves? It would certainly be our test of Mutterrecht sincerity.

Family is a natural energy *social state*. Most familiar are families of people. But there are families of: microbes, elements, energy forms, and even the forces of nature. People nesting in new worlds *sense* that complex beings observe them, while remaining hidden.

Family survival, well-being, and cohesion ultimately depend on mothers, and guiding matriarchs. Matriarch cultures, societies, families, clans, and tribes existed and thrived long before, and long after, patriarchs amassed populations, nations, and empires.

Freedom from patriarch tyranny benefits women, mothers, children, and all life. Limiting population curbs: pollution, abuse of nature, violence, exploitation, and victimization. The Cataclysm put an end to the toxic patriarch legacy. Now all life can benefit.

As we nest in the Cosmos, our post-Cataclysm legacy revives Mutterrecht, matriarch nurture, and matriarch longevity. A new and improved humanity is becoming *Gyna cosmos sapiens*. All indications are that we're headed toward cosmic fulfillment.

Humanity is at peace with the Cosmos, with each other, with life, and with Ma, Mother-Nature. Our creative energy is devoted to nurturing people and the cosmic life we encounter. We explore, tunnel, and nest in new worlds. *We easily take life, but we take it!*

*

Lela asked her training group of twelve pre-puberty kids to search the archives dealing with the transition from the Gold and Silver matriarch ages, to the Bronze and Iron of patriarchs. In particular, how did Bronze Age patriarchs change the family?

A warm cycle brought Earth the Great Flood, some 15,000 years ago. Earth released waters that washed-away most all critters. Surviving land life adapted to radically altered habitats. Yet some few people found the high ground or we wouldn't be here.

Survivors had mental and genetic advantages over non-survivors. Most significant, their kids survive thru us. Genetic changes to Great Flood survivors must have been favorable. At first, body chemistry favored human reproduction, for both gals and guys.

Fertile matriarchs would naturally remain ascendant for thousands of years, as they had been before the Great Flood. The end of the Neolithic and start of the Bronze Age saw a growing population of increasingly aggressive male leaders, the patriarchs.

With these comments, Lela suggests the kids look up in WikiArchives the words: Pandemic, Bronze, Iron, and Stone Ages. The Bronze dates from about 6,000 years before the present. Y'all will see Wiki references to 3,200 BC (Before the Common era).

Gold and Silver Ages are the first Mutterrecht matriarch periods. Matriarch humanity begins with primates before hominids. So-called *Modern* people date back perhaps 250,000 years. That date is from the oldest near-modern human genetic bone DNA artifacts.

Matriarch fertility, Venus figures, and burial artifacts are of bone, clay, and stone, dating back perhaps 100,000 years. Explore *The Language of the Goddess* by Marija Gimbutas, 1989. Her book contains 2,000 figures of recovered and verified human artifacts.

Joseph Campbell, a co-worker in antiquities, wrote this foreword:

The message here is of an actual age of harmony and peace in accord with the creative energies of nature which anteceded the six thousand years of what James Joyce has termed the 'nightmare' from which it is time for this planet to wake.

Lela: "As James Joyce anticipated, the Cataclysm is the wake-up call for planet Earth. Patriarch archives considered the matriarch era, before the Bronze Age, to be a myth. With substantial evidence, Gimbutas reveals the reality of a Matriarch Age.

"Gimbutas reveals the matriarch era was dedicated to fertility. Ma, as Deep Mother-Nature and Mother-Cosmos was seen as supreme deity. Stone, bone, and clay artifacts reveal the era before the Bronze Age as a distinctly social-cultural era of matriarchs.

"For 1,000 years now, the matriarch Cosmos emerges from what James Joyce called the *nightmare.* He suggests the toxic patriarch era began with the Bronze Age and degenerated into World War I, 1914 to 1918. Joyce did not live to see the far worse that followed.

"James Joyce's 20th Century *Ulysses* is Leopold Bloom, explorer of mind, imagination, and subconscious. Bloom's day relates his thoughts as he encounters people and places in Dublin, Ireland. The Latinized name *Ulysses* is of Homer's Mycenaean *Odysseus*.

"Homer's epic myth is of a Bronze Age warrior chief, *Odysseus*. The oral poem was first written in the Hellenic patriarch era, many centuries after Homer's passing. *Odysseus* is symbolic of Bronze Age patriarch dominance and suppression of matriarchs.

"Before the Cataclysm, it was suggested that Homer may have been a matriarch poet. In Homer's *Odyssey* and *Iliad*, so-called heroes have many faults and few virtues. Odysseus is cunning and devious. Homer calls him *a man of twists and turns*.

"So what do y'all think James Joyce meant when he used the term *nightmare* to describe the 6,000 years before the 20th Century? Homer's patriarchs are less heroes and more devious psychopaths. They sacrifice children claiming various god-inspired pretexts.

"In the Iliad, Agamemnon sacrifices his eldest daughter Iphigenia. The pretext is that she is to marry Achilles. But the sacrifice at Aulis is to produce favorable winds for sailing toTroy.

"Y'all do well to study the *Odyssey* and *Iliad.* These poems present a narrow view of Bronze Age people. But that may be the point. Bronze Age patriarchs were portrayed as ignorant, murderous and limited. Bronze Age men often were presented as inhuman.

"It's been suggested that pre-Cataclysm patriarchs did not progress much beyond the Bronze Age. Like Joyce's Bloom, Ulysses most likely would have fit into the 20th or even the 21st Century patriarch mold. The war against women persisted into the 21st Century.

"These epics show how patriarchs victimized women. How did increasing *population* and *hormone* change effect the growing victimization of women? Explore this question over the next week and we'll discuss it at our next session. Look into WikiArchives."

Within a week, the kids had a HoloVid based on Homer's ancient Greek versions of *Odyssey* and *Iliad. Multi-trans* converts ancient Linear Greek into *MaSprek*, and at the same time creates a Multi-D HoloVid. MaSprek also integrates MindRecord mems.

Neuron plasm feeds HoloVids and *TelepathTracks* (TelTs) into minds via *MindRecord.* TelTs provide sleep-learning functions thru

WikDrones. TelTs telepathics provide language skills thru the WikArchive database. Telepathy traits are also acquired via TelTs.

Kids translating 3,500 year-old Hellenic Linear Greek are fascinated by the challenge. Archaic Linear Greek had no punctuation. Words and sentences are run-on. With few clues, breaks in words and sentences must be intuited by the translator.

Kids created the *Hearts of Bronze* HoloVid. It's about cultural genocide, silencing *Her-story* with *His-story*. Matriarchy is subjugated by Bronze Age patriarchy. Included is a Spartan battle-field porridge recipe of: pig's blood, barley flour, and vinegar.

The HoloVid portrays a world in transition. *Her-story* is voiced by victimized matriarch leaders, as their world is up-ended. Penelope and Helen of the *Odyssey* and *Iliad* provide imagined thoughts. Amazons, Sappho, Clytemnestra, and Lysistrata offer their stories.

These are just a few of the legendary women resisting patriarch tyranny. They share in memory survival thru the millennia of the patriarch *holocaust* of women. Modern legends are of matriarchs surviving both holocaust and Cataclysm to thrive in the Cosmos.

The HoloVid conclusion provides an alternate reality. Shortly before the Cataclysm, a series of increasingly more deadly viral pandemics decimated humanity. It's this viral pandemic that sets the world stage for patriarch fear and the asteroid Cataclysm.

*

Lela: "Y'all created a wonderful HoloVid. It rightly stresses the role of mothers and family in Mutterrecht self-preservation. Nurturing life on Earth earns our invitation to nest in the Cosmos. I think we have Cyano and plasm electrons, the Visitors, to thank.

"Visitors advance not just brain neuron adaptation, but sustain trillions of body cells, and hundreds of different cell types. They enable the metabolism of billions of energy reactions per second in every body cell. Visitor plasms are electron energy jugglers.

"Electrons, plasms, protons, ions, electro-mags, and the like, all provide the impetus for our cosmic energy dynamics. They are the energy messengers for Ma, Deep Mother-Cosmos. Electrons are our cosmic workaholics, perpetually recycling cosmic energy.

"We need to understand matriarch adaptive evolution as we progress into *Gyna cosmos sapiens*. The adaptation of life is a never ending process. The Cataclysm and a thousand years of nurturing don't begin to explain how we become a cosmic species.

"The Cataclysm rapidly advanced Mutterecht. And our maturing attitude toward nurturing life continues to advance. We do well to explore the specific factors involved, in addition to the Visitors, plasm electrons, and a variety of microbes, there are other factors:

"Foremost is the perseverance of mothers as they strive to preserve family. Mothers resisted as patriarchs constantly victimized the family to satisfy their power lust. In spite of the challenges to survival, matriarchs persevere, while patriarchs do not.

"As mentioned earlier, I was nurtured in an extended family with many *goddess-like* women kin. Along with spouses and cousins, they nurtured and cared for each other as the need arose. My memories are of a consistently loving extended family.

"Bonobos and chimpanzees are considered our closest primate relations. It's instructive to study the relations between gals and guys in these primates. WikiArchives provides detailed observation data going back at least 100 years before the Cataclysm.

"The roots of the human family may be seen in these primate data. In most observations, primate mothers are at the core center of virtually all observed groups. Closest gal relations radiate outward from the center. Guys spend most time outside the gal circle.

"Guys are outside the circle of gals, providing protection and resources. This describes the geometry of the human family from earliest Stone Age artifacts. Mother Goddesses, Venus figures found in burial sites support these primate family origins.

"Before the Cataclysm, patriarch leaders fabricated the *nuclear* family. To satisfy patriarch greed, most global families were fragmented into impoverished duets of a single mother and child. Yet mothers tried to preserve the essence of Mutterrecht.

"In the Cosmic Matriarch Diary: most surviving Elders report fond pre-Cataclysm extended-family memories. Data from single-mother nuclear families report negative memories. The stress of nurturing children and kin remains a major challenge.

"It's love, caring, and nurture that we now provide. Longhouses and tunnel-towns in many worlds link people and life. Our place in the Cosmos expands as we become *Gyna cosmos sapiens*. A *mothers' place in the Cosmos is now and will be everywhere!*

"In her cosmic wisdom, Ma, Mother-Nature preserves one-in-a-thousand, while recycling the energy of billions. Nine-of-ten Cataclysm survivors continue to be gals, for people and most life. Is it chance, adaptation, or cosmic geometry code?

"It seems Ma sent the Cataclysm to cleanse Earth of population, pollution, and patriarchs. That ten-million survive on Earth is a powerful message, as is 99% of Earth being Mother-Sea. For 1,000 years, keeping faith with Ma, we thrive throughout the Cosmos.

"It's part of Mutterrecht: nurturing life and recycling cosmic energy. Ma provides plasm electrons and Cyanobacteria to sustain our progress in the Cosmos. We believe that these are Ma's gifts. Is Ma's supreme cosmic creation the *Family as a Social State*?

"OrmNet wormhole Portals to many worlds encourage tunnel-towns. While we limit our numbers on Earth, an open invitation is extended to new worlds and galaxies. This is all part of cosmic Mutterrecht. Ma nurtures those who love and respect her.

"Could a patriarch-dominated humanity have reached out to the Cosmos, as have matriarchs? Would matriarchs nest in the Cosmos without a cataclysm? Such questions are better left to kids. What do y'all have to say?"

Jena: "In view of Schrödinger's probability theory, as soon as the Cataclysm arrived, so did alternate universes. In some there were no cataclysms. In others, solar or cosmic flares, novas, or magnetic-polar shifts occur. But here it's our Earth, our universe."

Lil: "At our core we're electro-magnetic and Cyanobacteria *build-outs*. Plasm electrons are basic forms of cosmic *matter*. In alternate universes, plasm electrons may be the only life form. In our universe, plasm electrons are the major energy foundation."

Isis: "That's largely the case in the Cosmos we know and love. The basic energy system in all life forms is electron transfer. There's many variations, but these are all forms of electro-magnetism. No exceptions are found, as yet. Can life exist without electrons?

"On Earth and in all nested worlds we find some form of Adensosine Tri Phosphate shifting electrons back and forth with Adenosine Di Phosphate (ATP↔ADP). Sometimes it's sulfate in place of or with phosphate in energy transfer and genetic code."

Lela: "Mutterrecht, the Cataclysm, and a thousand years have brought major changes to people. What's the vision y'all have for people in the next millennia? Let's discuss your visions at our next meeting, next week, same place and time.

"For now, use your flying-suits if you like. If y'all need flying suits, let me know and we'll issue them from our longhouse store. Let's check the latest extent of the tunnel expansion.

"Use your Eye-cams to track animal numbers and movement. I'll check the sun-moon drone programming. Also, include tunnel segment numbers as part of Eye-cam recordings. I plan to go thru all ten tunnel segments and circle back to our starting point.

"That's a ten-mile circle. If y'all spot anything unusual note the mile location for later review. Anyone needing to rest along the way please feel free to do so. We'll all share the rest stop."

Publications

The MATRIARCH DIARY, B. P. Meinhardt, Sci-Fi
Hope from the 27th Century, 2021

The MURDER PHILOSOPHER, B. P. Meinhardt, Sci-Fi
Stories of 23rd Century Survival, 2019

MATRIARCH CHRONICLES, B. P. Meinhardt, Sci-Fi
13 Stories of Survival in the 23rd Century, 2018

ANXIOUS in AMERICA, B. P. Meinhardt, Non-fiction
Life with Generalized Anxiety Disorder (GAD), 2017

MATRIARCH, B. P. Meinhardt, Sci-Fi,
Matriarchy after the Cataclysm, 2016

FAMILY SECRETS, B. P. Meinhardt, Non-fiction
Creating Humanity Family by Family, 2015

The AFGHAN QUEEN, B. P. Meinhardt, Non-fiction
An American Woman's Five Years in Afghanistan, 2014

MA SAVES UNIVERSE, B. P. Meinhardt, Sci-Fi,
Matriarchs Reach the Stars, 2013

MOTHER EARTH, B. P. Meinhardt, Sci-Fi Erotica, 2012

CINDERELLA'S HOUSEWORK, B. P. Meinhardt, Non-fiction
Families in Crisis, Households in Chaos, 2010

CINDERELLA'S HOUSEWORK DIALECTICS, B. P. Meinhardt, Political economy of the family, economics doctoral thesis, 1977

www.ingramcontent.com/pod-product-compliance
Lightning Source LLC
LaVergne TN
LVHW012102160826

845678LV00014B/2907
9798370017810